Also by Ron Schwab

Sioux Sunrise
Paint the Hills Red
Ghosts Around the Campfire

The Lockes
Last Will
Medicine Wheel

The Law Wranglers
Deal with the Devil
Mouth of Hell
The Last Hunt
Summer's Child

The Coyote Saga
Night of the Coyote
Return of the Coyote

The Last Hunt

The Law Wranglers

Ron Schwab

Poor Coyote Press
OMAHA, NEBRASKA

Poor Coyote Press
P.O. Box 6105
Omaha, NE 68106
www.poorcoyotepress.com

Publisher's Note: This is a work of fiction. Names, characters, places, and incidents are a product of the author's imagination. Locales and public names are sometimes used for atmospheric purposes. Any resemblance to actual people, living or dead, or to businesses, companies, events, institutions, or locales is completely coincidental.

Ordering Information:
Quantity sales. Special discounts are available on quantity purchases by corporations, associations, and others. For details, contact the "Special Sales Department" at the address above.

The Last Hunt/ Ron Schwab -- 1st ed.

ISBN 978-1943421268

To Bev - the reason God made Oklahoma.

The Last Hunt

The Law Wranglers

1

JOSH RIVERS WALKED beside his father, Levi, as they strolled up the rocky path that wound its way to the top of the grassy knoll on which the cemetery was located. It was a late August afternoon, and the warming rays of an unclouded sun against his back were welcome and canceled out a cool breeze that swept off the mountains from the west. The cemetery plot that Levi had carved out of the hillside and fenced off with cedar posts and split logs had plenty of room for future occupants, and Josh assumed this would be his final resting place someday. For now, though, his late wife, Cassie, and mother, Aurelie, were the only persons buried in the family section. The graves of three cowhands, one of whom had been killed the same day as his wife and mother, were in an area further down the slope.

As they reached the top of the hill, the two men stopped in front of the crude crosses that marked the graves of their respective spouses. A man could see for a mile from this spot, Josh thought, follow the course of the clear stream that rushed over the rocks, as it snaked its way south through the lush valley and, at the same time, take in the breathtaking view of snow-capped mountains in the distance.

He had not visited the site for a year, and he chided himself for his neglect. He had travelled to the Slash R on at least three occasions in that time, and he wondered if he was avoiding the reminder of that dark day that changed his life forever. Still, he needed nothing to prompt his memory. It would be impossible to forget that day. He climbed the slope to the gravesite at his father's urging, and he had journeyed to the Slash R because he felt his father should receive more than a cold letter about Michael and Tabitha.

Josh studied the carefully carved words on the cross above his wife's grave: Cassandra Rivers. May 10, 1848-June 15, 1869. "I can't believe it's been over five years," Josh said, softly. He had loved her, as he had never loved a woman before or since, and her violent death had torn a hole in his heart that he expected would never be filled. Still, he recalled words he had read somewhere once:

"Don't grieve that it's over; smile that it happened."
He and Cassie had shared many moments he would not
have wanted to miss, if their paths had never crossed.

"Do you think your mom would be pissed about me
getting married again?" Levi asked.

The question came from out of nowhere, which was
not unusual during a conversation with Levi Rivers. He
generally said what he was thinking, and Josh never knew
for certain what that was. Pop had remarried less than
two months earlier at the same time as Josh's brother,
Cal, and because of a bizarre set of coincidences, Levi's
new bride, Dawn Rutledge, was the aunt of Cal's then
very pregnant bride, now Erin McKenna Rivers.

"Pop, Mom would be glad for you. Dawn's a fine woman, and Mom would want you to be happy," Josh lied. In
truth, Mom would probably be outraged. His parents'
marriage had often been a contentious one. Both were
stubborn and given to speaking their minds, and, while
they had carved out a life together, Levi's dawn till dark
work on the ranch likely gave them each welcome respite
from the other. Dawn, a dozen or so years younger than
Levi, had been lucky enough to encounter a sixty-eight-
year-old, mellowed Levi. It didn't hurt that she was a
calm, quiet, patient woman, either.

"You're a damn liar, Josh. I suppose it comes with being a law wrangler."

"Okay, Pop, neither of us knows what Mom would think. But you waited five years. It's time to get on with your own life."

"When you getting on with yours?"

"I am on with mine. Marriage just isn't part of it. Not now."

"You didn't ride all the way up here to make a cemetery visit. Tell me what you came for."

Josh looked at his father. He was still a vital man, standing ramrod straight at about six feet two inches, matching Josh's own height. He was more barrel-chested than Josh but otherwise lean and muscular. The thick white hair that creeped from the edges of his dusty Stetson had once been rust-colored like Josh's—and Michael's. The three also shared the same brown, green-flecked eyes.

"I wanted you to know that Cal and I made it back from Comanche country."

"A letter would have been fine. Hell of a thing, Calvin traipsing off with you the day after his wedding and missing the birth of his son."

"And I wanted you to hear from me that Tabby is okay."

"Did you bring her back? Why isn't she with you?"

"No." This is where it was going to get tough.

"Why the hell not? Where is she?"

"She's in Quanah's village. She's safe for now. We found her, but she refused to leave."

"Refused to leave? I don't understand."

"She wants to write a series of articles about the last days of the Comanche for the *Daily New Mexican*. And a book." Tabitha Rivers was a war correspondent for the daily newspaper during what she had dubbed the "Red River War" and had been taken captive by the Kwahadi band.

Levi shook his head from side to side in obvious disbelief. "What in the hell is it with that girl? She ought to be married and having babies by now. I shouldn't have sent her off to college in Denver. That gave her these damned crazy ideas about writing and taking dangerous chances. A book. I swear that girl got kicked in the head by a horse when she was up north."

"Pop, you didn't send her to school. She went. And like the rest of us, she paid her own way. She's twenty-two years old now and free to do what she damn well pleases. Her dispatches about the Red River War have made her famous. You should be proud."

Levi shrugged. Josh knew that his father was proud of his risk-taking, talented daughter, but he wasn't likely to ever admit it.

"What about Michael? I guess you and Cal didn't find him."

"We did."

This got Levi's attention. "You did? Where is he? Why didn't you bring him with you? I can't believe it. Deep down, I thought we'd never see him again." Tears formed at the crinkled corners of his eyes.

"He's still with the Comanche, in the same village as Tabby. Sharing a tipi with his aunt and adopted mother."

"He is? And you just left him there?"

"We had no choice. Cal and I would both be dead if we had tried to take Michael with us. Besides, my son thinks he is Comanche, and he knows no mother other than She Who Speaks."

"She Who Speaks?"

"Her husband was with the raiders who hit the ranch and killed Mom and Cassie. He took Michael to She Who Speaks, who has raised him as her own. His Comanche father was killed a year or so ago."

"Good. He needed killing. So, the boy's been raised up as a savage?"

"Well, Pop, I suppose, the definition of 'savage' might depend on who is defining the word, but Michael has been introduced to our white culture."

"Culture. Now here's a highfalutin word for you. What do you mean by that?"

"She Who Speaks was a white captive herself. She's about Tabby's age, maybe a year or two older. Her father was a Jewish doctor, and her parents were killed during a Comanche attack when they were a part of a wagon train crossing the Staked Plains. Her name then was Jael Chernik. She has a knack for languages. Her parents were German immigrants, and she speaks German, English, Spanish, Comanche and Yiddish. She acts as an interpreter for Quanah, and is quite influential. She has been teaching Michael, whose Comanche name is Flying Crow, to speak English, and she and Tabby are going to start teaching him to write."

"His so-called mother is a Comanche Jew? Damnedest thing I ever heard of."

"Pop, I can't say much, but I knew this woman before I was aware she had Michael. She's an exceptional person. Very intelligent. I am having some dealings with Quanah—nothing dishonest, I promise. She has acted as my contact."

"But she never told you she had your son?"

"No. And it didn't make me happy when I found out. But, again, I can't do anything about it right now. I take comfort that she would protect Michael with her life and that Tabby's there to look after him, too."

"I hear Mackenzie's back in the field. Living with the Comanche ain't a safe place for anybody these days, red or white. Quanah's half white himself. Won't make any difference to soldiers what color somebody is."

"I know, Pop, but we know they're both alive, and I don't think the Comanche will harm them. Jael—She Who Speaks—will see to that."

"What's this Comanche Jew lady look like?"

"Dark, very beautiful. She could easily pass for half-blood Comanche. Why?"

"You seem much impressed with this young kidnapper. Don't let your heart get in the way of your good judgment, Son."

Josh moved to start back down the path. "I don't know what you're talking about, Pop. I'll stay overnight, and then I'll head back to Santa Fe in the morning. My partner's starting to grumble I'm never in the office."

2

TABITHA RIVERS DID not know what day it was, but she knew she had been with Quanah's band for several months, and the days were not so long and hot now. She guessed it would be mid-September. It occurred to her that Flying Crow's birthday would be September 30th, but, of course, the Comanche would not be aware of that, and she supposed they did not maintain a calendar that precise anyway. Usually Kwahadi time was referenced by seasons. She guessed, by that standard, Flying Crow was six autumns old. Odd, she thought, that she had so easily come to think of him by his Comanche name.

The Kwahadi had been on the move since Josh and Cal departed after the futile trip to retrieve her and Flying Crow from the Comanche band. She knew her brothers had been angered and frustrated by her refusal to leave with them and with their aborted effort to take Flying Crow. But there were countless stories here, and she would not be denied. And Jael would never have surrendered Flying Crow. Thankfully, her brothers had the good sense to see they should go and live to fight another day. She liked to think Josh took some comfort in knowing she was here with his son and that Jael was an exceptional mother. There would be time enough to sort out Flying Crow's future.

This morning Tabitha sat cross-legged in front of the tipi making notes in the diary she had salvaged after her capture. She used her own system of shorthand and symbols to compile a journal that would someday be digested and turned into a series of newspaper stories and, with any luck, a book. Jael, known among the Kwahadi as She Who Speaks, suddenly appeared, a look of concern on her face. "Have you seen Flying Crow?" she asked.

"Not for some time. He was playing warrior games with some of the other boys along the creek. When I last saw him, Flying Crow was scalping some invisible white man, as near as I could tell."

"Quanah says we must move again. There is a small body of bluecoats only a half day away. He is taking out a war party to delay them. Isa-tai and a few of the warriors will lead us to our next hiding place." Isa-tai was a medicine man, often referred to as a toad by Jael, because she disliked the man, and his squatty, bloated appearance resembled the little amphibian.

Tabitha got up and tossed her pencil and journal through the tipi opening and joined Jael to search out Flying Crow and the other boys. As they approached the creek, one of the boys known as Prairie Dog came scrambling up the creek bank. His dark eyes were wide, and he spoke with lightning speed to Jael. Tabitha was slowly gaining a limited Comanche vocabulary, but she could not grasp a word the boy was saying. It was obvious he was frightened and excited, though.

Jael turned to Tabitha, "Would you go back to the tipi and bring back my bow and quiver? Prairie Dog says that two Tonkawa warriors are chasing Flying Crow and another boy along the creek and away from the village. They are no doubt scouts for the soldiers."

Tabitha wheeled and raced back to the tipi while Jael headed at a trot in the direction Prairie Dog had pointed. Tabitha quickly retrieved Jael's weapons, looping the shoulder strap of the quiver over her shoulder. She snatched up her own skinning knife and tied the rawhide strip that was attached to the sheath about her waist before she ran out of the tipi and returned to where she had last seen Jael. Shielding her eyes from the sun with her hand, she picked up Jael's blurred form moving eastward along the creek bank. Tabby bolted after her friend. She was in prime physical condition and almost rail thin after weeks on the trail as a war correspondent and then, after her capture, enduring the daily rigors of Comanche life.

Jael stopped for a moment, and Tabby caught up with her. Jael snatched up the bow and plucked an arrow from the quiver which hung on Tabby's shoulder. "They escaped," Jael said, pointing northward, along the creek bank. "One of the people eaters follows. The other has given up chase and has no doubt ridden to warn the soldiers we know of their presence."

Tabby knew Jael was referencing the Tonkawa, member of a tribe that had a reputation for cannibalism. She saw Flying Crow and an older boy, who was more than ten paces ahead of him, racing their way, and an Indian clad in breechclout and plaid flannel shirt pursuing the boys and closing in on Flying Crow. The Tonkawa carried a rifle, but was focused on the boy and had apparently not caught sight of the approaching women yet. Jael darted ahead toward her son, Tabitha following close behind.

The Tonkawa finally caught up with Flying Crow, grabbed him by the hair, and started to drag him away. By this time the two women, partially hidden by some scrub willows above the creek bed were no more than fifty feet away. Jael screamed at Flying Crow in Comanche, and he fell to the ground, throwing the warrior off balance. Jael nocked an arrow as the Tonkawa released the boy and turned toward her, raising his rifle. An arrow plunged into his right shoulder, throwing him backward before he could fire his weapon. Instinctively, Tabitha had pulled another arrow from the quiver and instantly handed it to Jael. The Tonkawa turned to run just as another arrow drove into the back of his neck, and his knees buckled and he dropped to the rocky ground, his rifle clattering on the stones.

Flying Crow got up and ran toward his mother as his friend scrambled up the creek bank and headed for the village. There were no tears, but the boy greedily welcomed her embrace, as he flew into her arms. Tabitha, her hand clutching the handle of her skinning knife, approached the fallen Tonkawa. He had something that had captured her interest.

First, she knelt next to the man's body to confirm he was, indeed, dead. She worked a cartridge belt off his shoulder and tugged it out from under his chest. Then she picked up the rifle. Her eyes sparkled with delight as she perused the weapon. It was a Henry, one of the .44 rimfire caliber rifles manufactured for the Union army during the Civil War. She knew the firearm well because Pop possessed a Henry that he used only for target shooting on special occasions. He wouldn't allow her brothers to fire the gun, but spoiled brat that she was, Tabitha had wheedled several opportunities to test it. According to Pop, only a limited number of the weapons had been manufactured. The rifle's chamber held fifteen cartridges, and the Confederates called it "the rifle the Yankees load on Sunday and shoot all week." She wondered how the Tonkawa had come into a weapon like this—and in such pristine condition. It did not matter, she decided. This was her rifle now. The Comanche had confiscated her Winchester, but she would be damned if they would take this one without a fight. It struck her for only a moment that a dead man lay at her feet, and she was without remorse, interested only in the looting of his possessions. What was she becoming?

Tabitha rejoined Jael and Flying Crow, who had been waiting for her return. "You found something that pleases you," Jael observed.

"A Henry repeating rifle. Do you think they will let me keep it?"

"I cannot say. You are trusted now, but some will think only warriors should have a rifle."

"I am a warrior. I have fought and I have killed."

"Yes, but you have fought and killed Comanche."

Jael took the quiver from Tabitha's shoulder, and the young journalist quickly substituted the cartridge belt. "It's my rifle," she insisted. "You have your weapons."

"True. This was the bow of my husband, Four Eagles, and he taught me to use it, even though his other wives resented it."

As they strolled toward the village, Tabitha sensed another opportunity to learn more of her fascinating friend's history. Jael had spoken little about her marriage "You have told me before that your husband had two other wives. Didn't that bother you?"

"No, that is the way of the People. It is a practical necessity. Because of wars and the other risks that go with the man's role in the tribe, many die prematurely. There are more females than males of reproductive age. Polygamy is necessary to perpetuate the race and to provide for the care of the women, who would not otherwise have the care of a male provider and protector."

"I would rather protect and provide for myself than share a man."

"It is a matter of the society we live in."

"But you told me you refused to become your brother-in-law's fourth wife."

Jael shrugged and gave a small smile. "Even though I was my husband's favorite wife, I did not like sharing. The other two wives were jealous because he was most often in my robes. They complained, and he insisted he did so because I was unable to conceive, and it was his duty to be with me. I knew better. I learned what pleased him and how to make him want to pleasure me." Her eyes met Tabitha's, and they both giggled.

"And now you allow the People to think you are of two spirits—that you share your robe with another woman?"

"It protects you, and I am not presently interested in another man, so it is convenient. I have some skill with medicine that is useful to the band, and Quanah values my counsel and interpreting services, so meat is left outside my tipi from time to time, and I can hunt. Thus, I do not require a man to provide for me—but it might be nice on occasion to have one to pleasure me." Again, the women giggled.

3

TABITHA AND JAEL continued their light-hearted conversation as they neared the village, and Tabitha admitted to herself that their behavior was a bit bizarre after the turmoil and the killing of a man just minutes earlier. Flying Crow trailed along behind, uncharacteristically quiet and seemingly disinterested in the dialogue between the two young women. Suddenly, the roar of gunfire and screaming coming from the village broke the mood.

Jael shouted orders in Comanche to the boy, and he disappeared down the gentle slope of the creek bank to the dry bed that edged the feeble stream that threaded it. The women hurried ahead toward the anguished sounds.

When the women arrived at the edge of the village they found a melee of women and children in the process of being herded like balky cattle near the center of the encampment by mounted soldiers. Bodies of women, old and young, bearing angry, scarlet slashes across necks and arms as torsos were strewn about the village grounds. Several dead children, and even a bawling baby, were interspersed among the corpses.

Jael and Tabitha stood on slightly higher ground no more than forty feet upslope from the small village when they were spotted by a soldier who wheeled his horse and charged toward them with upraised saber. Tabitha lowered herself to one knee, raised her new rifle to her shoulder, chambered a cartridge, aimed and fired. A hole in the middle of the soldier's forehead erupted blood, and he plunged from the horse. Another soldier, who had followed his comrade, slipped from his mount with Jael's arrow plunged deeply in his chest.

Tabitha observed a soldier emerging from Doe Watcher's tipi wrestling with his trousers which were seemingly locked about his knees. He was not an immediate threat, so she placed two bullets in his buttocks. He screamed and stumbled to the ground.

Jael had charged into the encampment, but Tabitha judged she could be more effective from her current vantage point. She caught sight of the squat Isa-tai fending off a burly soldier's bloody blade with his war club. The soldier evidently tired of the game and drew his sidearm from its holster, aiming it at the medicine man. Tabitha fired again and delivered bullets to the soldier's hip and ribs before Isa-tai leaped forward and dropped him with a stout blow from the war club to the man's temple. The medicine man looked her way and was obviously surprised to see Tabitha with her rifle. He raised the war club to her in salute. She nodded her acknowledgement. There could have been no more than a dozen soldiers, a scouting expedition of some kind she guessed, and they seemed to be confused by the sudden resistance, and the women had begun to fight back with hatchets and lances and any object that might do damage. Isa-tai and one of the warriors who had remained behind began to organize the survivors, and the hapless soldiers, some of whom were wounded by Tabitha's bullets or Jael's arrows, were pulled from their horses and angrily swarmed by the women and older children.

Tabitha could see that the massacre had been reversed, and she got up and walked into the village, heading immediately for Doe Watcher's tipi. She entered and found her friend lying on her buffalo robe, her eyes staring vacantly into space and her skirt lifted above her waist revealing her naked and bloody mound. Her throat had been raggedly slashed. Tabitha could not fight back the tears that rolled down her cheeks. Doe Watcher had been one of her early friends who had been delighted when Tabitha gave her some under garments that had so fascinated the young Comanche woman. She was a pretty, although somewhat thick-waisted, maiden with a kind and cheery disposition. Doe Watcher was known throughout the village as a craftswoman of moccasins and animal skin apparel, and she had repaid Tabitha with the young reporter's first pair of moccasins.

Uncertain what she was going to do to the perpetrator she had taken down, she exited the tipi to confront him. She was too late. One of the women was holding her skinning knife in one hand and the man's testicles in the other, while Isa-tai sliced away a scalp, seemingly oblivious to the soldier's uncontrollable sobbing. Tabitha turned away and left to find Jael and Flying Crow.

By the time Quanah and his war party returned several hours later, the dead had been wrapped in skins and laid side by side and the tipis had been dismantled and the belongings packed on horses and travois. There was no time for mourning, and the spirits of their friends and loved ones would have to find their ways to the afterlife, with the Great Spirit's guidance, from these stark and empty plains.

As she helped Jael ready their own tipi and belongings for the journey, the reality struck that she had killed soldiers of her own people. Did that make her a renegade or traitor? Mention of her part in the incident might best be left unwritten.

4

JOSH AWAKENED BEFORE sunrise. He lay 4quietly and unmoving in the darkness, taking care not to disturb the naked woman whose soft, rhythmic breathing he found calming. They had spent the night in Jessica Chandler's room at the Exchange Hotel, where they both resided, his own rooms being located conveniently at the opposite end of the hall.

He had arrived early evening on his return to Santa Fe and had seen a light on in the Teatro Santa Fe, the theatre managed by Jessica, which was quickly becoming the blossoming city's cultural center. He had stopped by to be welcomed by Jessica's warm embrace and a promise of greater things if he would bathe and shave and take her to a late dinner at the La Castillo. She was a lady of her word.

He had first encountered Jessica on the Staked Plains, where members of a traveling theatre company aboard a single stagecoach were under attack by a small band of Comanche. Josh had chased off the attackers, but he had been too late to save the three male thespians, one of whom was Jessica's husband. It turned out that Jessica and her husband, a man twenty years older than her thirty-five years, had endured a long and contentious relationship and her mourning lasted no more than a half day. The next morning, Jessica and Josh, naked in their shared bedroll, had been captured by Quanah and a small war party, which led to his first meeting with She Who Speaks, the war chief's interpreter and counselor. And now She Who Speaks, also known as Jael Chernik, had thrust herself into his life in ways he could never have imagined.

Josh decided he should return to his room at a discreet hour and slipped out of the blankets and swung his legs over the side of the bed. He started when he felt Jessica's hand on his shoulder.

"Don't leave yet," she said. "I have something to tell you."

His first thought was that she was pregnant, although she had assured him that she only took a lover at what she called "safe times," whatever those were. Also, she thought she was unable to conceive, having had, she said, many opportunities to do so,

"What do you want to tell me?"

"Lie down next to me."

He obeyed, and she nestled into his arms, her nipples brushing against his chest and her soft hair tickling his cheeks. He felt an awakening in his loins that he had not intended. "Now tell me."

"It's time for us to take a break."

"A break? From what?"

"Getting together like this."

"I don't understand. Why?"

"You acted guilty last night. Like your mind was somewhere else. With another woman, perhaps."

"I didn't please you?"

"Of course, you pleased me. I've never had a better lover. And I have never asked questions or demanded that I be your exclusive lover. God knows you're not mine."

The last remark stung a bit, although he had always suspected its truth. Expecting a woman with Jessica's enthusiasm for frolic to remain chaste during his long absences was likely not realistic, but sometimes a man would rather not know. And after all, since his falling out with Constanza Hidalgo not quite a year back, Jessica had been his only lover. He liked women, but he did not think of himself as a promiscuous man. His and Jessica's tight friendship had made their physical relationship special. "There is no other woman in my life, and, anyway, you just said that you have never demanded that we be exclusive to each other, so why would it matter?"

"A woman has touched your life in a different way. I can sense it, even if you don't know it . . . or won't admit it. You need some time to sort things out. Our break doesn't have to last forever. But if it does, we'll still have our friendship. I don't want to risk that."

"You're the strangest damn woman I've ever run up against."

"That's the idea."

He could feel her fingertips dancing down his abdomen, teasing him to a frenzy. "You don't suppose?" he said.

"I suppose," she replied, laughing and pulling him tightly against her warm and welcoming flesh.

5

I T WAS NOT yet seven o'clock when Josh arrived at the
Rivers and Sinclair offices, the earliest he could remember ever showing up for work. Danna Sinclair
was already in the office, though, so he forfeited any
bragging rights. He walked down the dusky hallway to
Danna's office, saw that her door was open, and tapped
lightly on the doorframe. "Danna, do you have time to
talk a few minutes?"

Danna, apparently startled, looked up from some papers spread out on her desk. She smiled with that enchant-
ing smile that had a way of breaking down the toughest
barriers and abruptly lifted herself from her chair and
rushed across the room to greet him with a quick, chaste
hug, before offering her cheek for an equally brief and
decorous kiss. She stepped back, hands still resting gently on his shoulders and her sparkling sapphire-blue eyes

met his eyes and made him feel genuinely welcome. Over five feet ten inches tall, Danna didn't yield much height to a man who was barely four inches taller and certainly would not have been intimidated by a giant. Stunningly beautiful, with strawberry blonde hair and a quick incisive mind, Danna acted as the firm's managing partner, even though she was just a few months short of twenty-five years of age.

Josh, as the senior partner, was only four years older, but he had founded the firm and taken Danna in after they combined efforts on a captive child case that had eventually triggered the chain of events that led him to his own son. Josh, however, was rarely in the office and didn't have a taste for the day-to-day decision making, and he had quickly surrendered management to Danna, who eased naturally into the boss's role.

Danna moved toward her desk. "Sit down, Josh. I haven't seen you for more than a month. Tell me why you decided to show up in Santa Fe," she teased.

Josh took no offense. Danna kept a close eye on the books, and she was aware that Quanah's gold was the firm's single largest source of income. He told her of his and his brother Cal's trek to the Kwahadi village and their discovery that their sister, Tabby, and his son, Michael, were both ensconced in Jael Chernik's tipi.

"This is almost more than I can absorb at one telling," Danna said. "So, Tabby's not really a captive?"

"I don't know what she is. She evidently wants to stay... thinks she's collecting a treasure of newspaper articles and the makings of a book. She asked me to let the *Daily New Mexican* know that she's alive and assumes she's still on their payroll, but I cannot say much else without divulging our professional involvement. Cal said I could attribute any reports to him, which would be credible because of his history as an Army scout. While I'm convinced Tabby wants to stay, I don't think Quanah would permit her to leave. She knows too much."

"And Michael? You must feel very conflicted."

"I do. There is the joy of knowing he's alive. Then there is the sadness of realizing that in his own mind he is a Comanche and that She Who Speaks ... Jael ... is his mother. I would not be speaking with you now if Cal and I had tried to take him with us, so I can only wait until the Kwahadi come to the reservation."

"Then they will be forced to surrender Michael, won't they?"

"Yes."

"You don't seem all that excited."

"And he will be taken from the only mother he's ever known. Someone who has been a devoted mother. A woman who is extremely intelligent and sensitive, and quite exceptional, I must admit."

"And quite attractive, I take it."

Josh saw a twinkle in Danna's eyes that annoyed him a bit. "She is that, but her looks don't make her a good mother."

"No, of course not."

Josh removed a black feather from his coat pocket and handed it to Danna, who studied the object with a perplexed look on her face. "It's a feather," she announced, stating the obvious.

"A crow feather, to be exact. Michael's Comanche name is Flying Crow. He gave me this just before I left the village. I'm keeping this as hope that we'll be together again, that he will accept me as his father, and that we will work this out some way."

Danna returned the feather. "You will. That's what we lawyers do . . . we find ways."

Josh quickly changed the subject. "How is Marty Locke working out?" Locke was a former Confederate officer Danna had employed to handle the firm's trial work. He was about Josh's age with Virginia roots. Josh didn't know the entire story, but Martin Locke's wife and daughter had died before he came west and landed in Santa Fe.

"He's partner material. An excellent, disciplined lawyer. Of course, you would expect that from a University of Virginia graduate."

Danna had also graduated from the University of Virginia. Josh, the outsider, had been educated at Hastings College of Law in California. Most western lawyers had travelled the law clerking route of "reading the law" and taking the bar examination to earn their ways to the profession. Josh had found no discernible difference in quality between the college and self-educated lawyers except, perhaps, occasional snobbishness on the part of the more formally schooled counselors.

Josh said, "I'm glad he's working out. When we last spoke, you said we might need yet another lawyer."

"Probably two eventually. But I think at some point we limit our growth. I don't want us to get so large we get fat with bureaucracy and fail to give our clients personal attention. I hope you agree."

"I do. I'm glad you feel that way. I was starting to get a little nervous about hiring lawyers so quickly."

"The work's there, but we're already turning down cases if we can't take care of them properly. We'll just have to be selective."

"Speaking of more lawyers. I have something I want to propose. I touched on this briefly another time."

"Tell me about it."

"I would like to open another office near Fort Sill and the Comanche reservation. My guess is that the Kwahadi will be on the reservation in less than a year."

Danna lifted her eyebrows, obviously surprised, but not otherwise expressing an opinion. "Go on."

"Quanah is our best client, and he is going to need legal help for many years. He is only one of many Comanche chiefs, but he has excellent political skills and rare insight. He's a young man in his mid-twenties, and I would bet he's going to become the acknowledged leader and spokesman for the entire Comanche nation in a matter of a few years. I don't think his resources are unlimited, but he has a stash of gold he's paying us from, and I assure you he won't be turning that over to the army."

"So, you don't think our relationship with Quanah ends with his surrender?"

"Not if we don't want it to."

"And where would we find a lawyer to run that office?"

"I would be responsible for it. I wouldn't have to be there full-time. I will try to convince Jael Chernik to manage the office and start reading the law with the goal of passing the bar exam someday. She won't abandon the Comanche, and Quanah will continue to look to her for counsel anyway. Why don't we let her provide this counsel as a member of our firm?"

"How can you be certain Quanah is going to be so influential?"

"I admit this is something of a gamble. But my gut tells me he is not an ordinary man. Regardless, there are few lawyers in the entire country with expertise in the matters of Indian treaties and reservation law. The legal status of Indians is even ambiguous. Are they citizens, with full constitutional rights? We can open up a new area of practice and face very little competition, certainly not until after we've gained a dominant position."

Danna shook her head doubtfully. "You made a place for me in this firm. You established the office. I don't see how I could object."

"But your approval is important to me. We are partners."

Danna smiled. "You've got my approval. Frankly, I'm intrigued by the idea."

"Good. Now I've got to convince Jael."

"She will be suspicious. And I assure you she won't barter Michael for this opportunity."

"No, Michael will remain an issue between us. When I have the Army remove him from tribal custody, the whole plan could blow up, as far as she's concerned.

But pursuing this area of practice near the reservation makes sense. Remember, other Comanche bands are there along with Arapaho, Cheyenne and Kiowa."

"I agree. Without your She Who Speaks, the Fort Sill office still makes sense."

6

WHITE WOLF WAS growing tired of the chase. His contract as a civilian scout for the Army was set to expire in a month, and he had no intention of signing on for another military expedition. September was drawing to an end now, and he had been in the field with Colonel Ranald Slidell Mackenzie's Fourth Cavalry for several months, since returning from an aborted effort to rescue Tabitha Rivers, who did not want to be rescued, from Quanah's Kwahadi band.

During his rescue attempt, Wolf had been wounded by a small Comanche boy who drove a crude lance beneath his shoulder. He had narrowly escaped and was later found and nursed to recovery by the legendary Indian fighter and cattleman, Charles Goodnight. At the time, Goodnight had been scouting the southern portion of the Palo Duro Canyon for ranching prospects. He stayed with Goodnight for several weeks and was dubbed "Oliver Wolf" by his friend, who insisted he required a civilized name if he was going to make a living in Santa Fe as Wolf planned.

While with Goodnight, Wolf had a chance encounter with Josh and Cal Rivers, who were on a mission to recover their sister, Tabitha, and Josh's son. They had politely declined his offer to join them. Wolf had heard nothing about Tabitha's rescue, and he suspected the foolhardy brothers' scalps now decorated some Comanche lances. Perhaps he could learn something of their fate when he went to Santa Fe. He thought often of Tabitha with whom he had become good friends during the course of her tour as a war correspondent prior to her capture.

Wolf led his big gelding along the rim of the Palo Duro Canyon, his eyes searching for signs of Comanche or Kiowa. He was at the northern end of the canyon, a good one hundred miles north of where he and Goodnight had scouted. Wolf thought the place was too expansive to be called a canyon, yet he didn't know what label might be attached to it. The Prairie Dog Fork of the Red River snaked its way through the canyon floor, which was probably a thousand feet below the overhanging rim. He guessed that the canyon was about ten miles wide at this spot, sighting west from where he stood, but at other points it might be as much as twenty miles or as short as a mile across.

He walked southward, taking care to keep some distance from the treacherous, and often unstable, ledge that overlooked the canyon. He paused, as he thought he saw midway across the canyon several columns of smoke swirling upward before fanning out and disappearing. His eyes focused on the area near the ribbon of water that meandered through the wild cherry, juniper, mesquite and cottonwood that blocked his view of the canyon floor. He waited patiently for some minutes and was finally rewarded with more tufts of smoke.

He continued his trek, never losing sight of the spot where he had picked up the smoke. Finally, he came to a goat trail that appeared to drop over the canyon's edge and head to the river below. It was too narrow and dangerous for the horse, which was probably just as well, since he needed to make this journey quietly. It was nearly dusk, and the fading of daylight would slow his descent, but he was less likely to be observed by a Comanche sentry under cover of darkness. He staked out the gelding near a patch of dry, but edible, grass and then slipped through a fissure in the rocky rim and picked up the trail. He found the path well-worn and easy enough to follow, but he had to hug the canyon wall from time to time to avoid stepping off into the nothingness that would carry him to his death on the rocks below.

When he reached the canyon floor, he disappeared into the brush and moved silently and steadily in what he estimated to be the direction from which the smoke had come. He did not have to walk as far as anticipated. No more than two miles from the canyon's east edge he came upon a Comanche encampment. He walked around it and soon he came upon another and, later, another. Before he returned to his goat trail, he had found five villages with several hundred lodges. He had also discovered huge herds of horses near the village, a sure indication these nomads of the plains were settled in for the winter. Horses were the Comanche's life blood and measure of wealth. For security, when bands were on the move the remuda would be dispersed.

It was nearly sunrise when Wolf climbed onto the canyon's rim. His job was to report what he had seen to Colonel Mackenzie immediately. Allowing for stops to rest and water his mount, he figured the former brevet general was nearly a full day distant. What he had witnessed was significant, but he loved horses, and he would not ride his gelding to its death.

7

MACKENZIE WAS ELATED when Wolf delivered the news of his discovery of the Comanche villages. The commanding officer had chased Comanche in Palo Duro Canyon on other military expeditions, and no soldier knew the canyon's terrain and hidden entrances and exits as well as the seasoned Comanche fighter. He ordered the buglers to sound "boots and saddles" even though nightfall was coming on.

Wolf, who had not slept for over twenty-four hours, was ordered to accompany Colonel Mackenzie and lead the soldiers to the location of the Comanche. Selecting a fresh horse from the remuda, he rode with the "General," as most soldiers called him in deference to his civil war brevet rank. He found himself dozing in the saddle, but it did not seem to perturb Mackenzie, who was absorbed in discussing strategy with his officer. Wolf did not enjoy the colonel's company and found him arrogant and obsessive. He looked more like a ruffian than a military officer and usually smelled like rotting carrion. However, he had the utmost respect for the man as a soldier. Mackenzie was a brilliant strategist, and his obsessive traits drove him to unparalleled determination and persistence in pursuit of his quarry.

When Mackenzie and his seven companies of Fourth Cavalry arrived at Palo Duro Canyon's edge and were shown the location of the Comanche villages, Wolf was dismissed. He did not protest. He was tired of chasing and fighting the damn Comanche. He considered himself Cherokee, despite his healthy infusion of Scottish blood and a bit of Tonkawa, and his folks had no personal quarrel with the Comanche or Kiowa. He was also certain Quanah and the Kwahadi would not be found in the canyon and that this was not the band that held Tabitha captive.

One company of the Fourth remained above the canyon as Mackenzie and his other scouts ferreted out a trail that would lead the others to the canyon floor. While the soldiers made their descent into the canyon, Wolf chatted with Sergeant O'Hara, a white-haired, melon-bellied man, who was not disappointed at being left behind.

"Ain't going to surprise anybody with all the noise they're making going down that wall," the sergeant said. "Sounds like a herd of buffalo going over the edge."

"I agree. I'm amazed they haven't been spotted. The Comanche must feel safe there."

"They're going to find out soon enough. And they're going to learn about the new strategy."

"What new strategy?"

"Starve 'em out."

"What do you mean?"

"Cut off their food supplies. Take their horses. New orders have come out to find and watch what's left of the buffalo herds and chase the red devils away from them." Apparently remembering that Wolf would be considered a "red devil," he added quickly, "No offense meant."

Wolf ignored the remark. "They'll find other herds and game."

"Not without horses."

"I don't understand."

"The new order says to kill their horses."

Their conversation was suddenly interrupted by the sounds of gunfire and screams and chaos rising from the canyon floor. A green lieutenant ordered the troops to spread out along the canyon's rim, a useless effort, Wolf thought, given that the fighting was so distant they could not identify a target from this range, let alone hit anything. They took up such a tiny segment of the canyon wall, there was not much chance they would confront escaping Comanche. He was curious, though, and slipped away and located a likely trail and commenced his own slow and cautious descent into the canyon.

He walked and sometimes slid his way on the parched dirt and rocks that lined the canyon walls. Half way down he paused and studied the scene that was unfolding. Women and children were running for the canyon walls like ants racing from a destroyed anthill, finding winding trails and paths unseen by the white enemy. There were hundreds of them scaling the steep walls and disappearing into cracks and crevices. Others led pack horses away, apparently heading toward secret exits that would permit them to salvage both animals and belongings. The warriors, of course, carried on the fight with the soldiers so their families could elude the enemy, but soon Wolf caught sight of clusters of warriors reaching the walls. They inched their ways upward, turning intermittently and firing down on their attackers, giving the women and children yet more time. Wolf assumed that the retreat was taking place throughout the canyon, and the Comanche resistance seemed more token than real at this point.

The soldiers did not seem to be giving serious chase and soon turned back to the interior of the canyon. By the time Wolf completed his descent, countless columns of thick, black smoke were curling skyward, casting a gray blanket over the lower levels of the canyon, which a few hours earlier had been bathed in mid-morning sunlight. He could hear the frantic whinnying of horses to the south, and the loud chorus told him soldiers must be rounding up a massive herd. It would take days for the Army to get a large herd of horses out of the canyon without driving them some miles south, he thought. The trails at this end were too narrow to move a mass of animals up the steep walls.

He saw his Tonkawa cousin, Rattlesnake, walking toward him, leading a chestnut gelding and gray mare by braided rawhide ropes attached to their halters, which were doubtless looted from the fleeing Comanche. Rattlesnake had recruited Wolf, a former major in the First Cherokee Brigade of the Confederate army, to scout for Mackenzie. Wolf had taken up carpentry and masonry as a trade to subsidize his ambitions as an artist. His future had not looked promising in Arkansas, and he had headed for Santa Fe. Stopping to visit his mother's relatives in the Indian Territory, he encountered Rattlesnake, and the scouting money and steady meals appealed to the former soldier, who had found himself nearly destitute midway on his journey across the seemingly endless prairie.

He raised his hand in greeting. "Rattlesnake, you have become a man of property, I see."

"Cousin, happy to see you. Bad Hand Mackenzie say scouts claim two horses before sun high in sky." Rattlesnake pointed straight upward, Wolf took this to mean noon, which was probably an hour away. He and his cousin generally communicated by English because Rattlesnake's rudimentary English was better than Wolf's Tonkawa.

"The General's giving away Comanche horses?"

"Only scouts get horses. Others get killed. Go. Get horses now. Me see you canyon top." Rattlesnake pointed south along the canyon wall and moved on with his bounty.

Wolf was not clear on what his cousin was telling him, but he had an ominous feeling. He angled back to the wall, and, as he followed it southward, the frantic sounds of crazed horses and yelling, cussing men filled the air. A half hour later the canyon wall abruptly turned east and after less than quarter of a mile turned back again, ultimately shaping an enormous dead-end branch canyon packed with stomping, twisting horses, held within its confines by more than a hundred soldiers, many with ropes in their hands and others with rifles. He walked over to a young lieutenant he had ridden with and who seemed to be supervising the natural corral.

"Lieutenant. What's happening, sir?"

"You've got less than half an hour to pick two horses, White Wolf. I'll send a couple of men with ropes along with you. Make your picks fast. The General will chew my ass if we don't get started by noon."

"Get started with what, sir?"

"The killing. Orders are to kill every horse."

Wolf could not imagine. Surely they would not follow through with this insanity. But his immediate instinct was to save two. There were hundreds from which to choose. He moved quickly toward the fringes of the herd. It would be death to walk into the hoofed melee of frightened beasts. His eyes fastened on a muscular, black stallion with irregular white rings encircling his eyes like broken spectacles. He could swear the horse's large, fiery eyes were locked on his. He pointed to the horse and one of the soldiers hurried to rope the stallion.

He continued his trek along the edge of the trapped horses. Ordinarily, he would have been satisfied with the fine horse he had selected, but if the Army should go forward with its foolishness, he had an opportunity to rescue another victim. He spotted a gray filly with a spattering of white spots on her rump—perhaps, a bit of Appaloosa blood, he guessed. She was young and pretty, not standards by which a true horseman should make a choice, but it was love at first sight, and he signaled his selection to the other soldiers.

He walked backed to the lieutenant and waited for the soldiers to bring his selections to him. He chose from a nearby stack of Comanche halters two that he decided should fit his acquisitions. The lieutenant told him to take his pick of the braided lead ropes since the army wouldn't be needing them.

When the soldiers brought him the roped horses, he calmed the animals and haltered them and attached the lead ropes with little problem. The Comanche were superior horsemen, and the horses, even the filly, would have been handled often.

"You will want to be on your way," the lieutenant said softly, "before your horses get too skittish. We must commence carrying out our orders."

Wolf turned and saw soldiers pulling a dozen roped horses from the massive herd to the outer mouth of the canyon. They began lining up the animals and staking them, anchoring the horses' heads snugly with their noses no more than a foot from the ground. As the soldiers dispersed, twenty others armed with the powerful Sharps rifles marched forward and lined up about twenty-five feet from the row of horses. A firing squad, he thought, in disbelief.

A sergeant yelled out the order to fire and the guns roared. Not a single horse dropped, although they fought to break free, and several screamed in panic. Wolf's stare was fixed on the wild, frightened eyes of the horses, knowing the sight would haunt him forever. Obviously, every soldier had deliberately fired his weapon above the condemned.

The lieutenant marched angrily out to the sergeant and was obviously ripping his ass without mercy. Then the lieutenant stalked back to his position. The sergeant yelled at the troopers, "Court martial for every one of you cowardly bastards if they don't go down this time. Do your duty."

The orders issued again and the rifles answered, and this time horses fell, some instantly dead, others flailing helplessly, shrieking in fear and pain. Some of the soldiers reloaded and moved closer to complete the killing of the survivors.

Wolf turned, unashamed of the tears that streamed down his cheeks, and led his own horses away, heading northward, as far away from this slaughter as he could get. He was anxious to find an exit from the canyon that would allow him to remove his rescued creatures from this forever blighted place. The sickening sounds of gunfire and screaming animals followed him the remainder of the day as he climbed a narrow trail out of the canyon and led his horses over the rim and onto the flat plains. The steady cracking of the rifles continued until after sundown. Wolf could not bring himself to eat that night, and after tending to his gelding and his new stallion and filly, he spread out his bedroll and futilely tried to sleep. At sunrise, the rhythm of the slaughter took up again.

8

"QUANAH HAS SUMMONED me," Jael said. "I am told it is urgent." She had pulled back the tipi flap and peered in to find Tabitha and Flying Crow absorbed in the boy's lessons.

"We are working on his reading and writing today," Tabitha replied. "Do you object if I teach him to write his birth name? I've taught him to write his Comanche name."

Jael hesitated. She was still loath to admit he had ever been known as anyone but Flying Crow. But it was time. "That would be fine," she said, before closing the flap and heading for Quanah's lodge.

As she weaved among tipis toward the far end of the village, she surveyed the encampment where they had found tolerable safety for more than a month now. Tipis stretched from wall to wall of the shallow canyon that merged with the mighty Palo Duro to the north. It was said that nearly five hundred of the People had gathered here now, mostly Kwahadi bands of the Comanche but also a few Kiowa bands and some stray Cheyenne from the northern plains. There was an ample water supply, but wild game was getting scarcer, and hunting parties were venturing further into the big canyon where more deer and remnants of scattered buffalo herds were wintering. With the huge gathering of the People here, the food sources would not last the winter. She estimated they would be eating horses before the snows ended. By the white man's calendar, she figured the month of October had passed by now.

She approached Quanah's tipi. The tall war chief, who dwarfed most Comanche with his stature, stood outside, staring trance-like up at the azure, cloudless sky as if seeking answers from a source that dwelt there. Perhaps, he was drawing strength from the radiant sun that brought unseasonable warmth to the midday. His face seemed old and troubled for a man in his mid-twenties.

Quanah turned and faced her as she drew nearer and signaled for her to follow him into the tipi. His two wives were busy with chores near the glowing coals of a dying fire and seemed to take no notice of her. Their presence reminded Jael that she had tactfully evaded Quanah's suggestion, following her husband's death, she would be welcome as a third wife. She had not found the thought of warming his robe unpleasant, for he was a strikingly handsome and seductive man. Sharing him with others was not appealing, however. She had already been a warrior's third wife. And she was not prepared to surrender the status, influence and freedom she had earned and would inevitably lose if she became his wife.

They sat on a buffalo robe facing each other, and, speaking Comanche, Jael said, "You asked that I come here, Chief Quanah."

"Yes, She Who Speaks, it is time we talk of the seasons that are coming. Our way of life is ending. Many of the chiefs do not believe this. They want to fight on and believe foolishly that the white eyes will tire and go away. This will not happen. The People here will be hungry as winter sets upon us, and by the season of awakening, we will be weak and desperate. We must prepare for the surrender."

"Yes, you are wise. We must prepare for this."

"They killed horses, not for food, because the animals were left for the vultures and coyotes and other eaters of carrion."

"I do not understand."

"Many suns to the north . . . in this very canyon . . . Mackenzie and his soldiers killed over thirteen hundred Comanche horses."

"Why would they do this?"

"So the People cannot hunt or provide for themselves. So the People are without wealth. This is very cruel and a great waste. And it is very smart. I do not want our horses killed unless it is necessary to feed the People."

"You wish me to do something. What would you have me do?"

"You must find Rivers and tell him we are ready to come in. I cannot promise that all will follow. I am only one chief among many in this village. I will try to persuade the others, and I will ask all who are willing to come with me. Those numbers will grow as the winter reveals our plight."

"Are there terms?"

"We are at their mercy. But these are the terms I want Rivers to put forth: Our chiefs will not be imprisoned as others have. Our horses will not be killed, and we will be provided cattle that we can care for ourselves in the white man's way. And we will sign no papers. We will have nothing to do with this thing they call a treaty. Tell Rivers that I will work with the white eyes and seek to become the acknowledged leader of all the People. Remind him that my mother was a white woman. Tell him I will take the name of my mother's people and will be known to all as Quanah Parker."

It was obvious Quanah had been thinking about this for some time and that he did not plan to be a meek "reservation Indian" standing in line for his daily food allotment. He was planning to step into a new world and chart his own destiny. She knew if anyone could accomplish that it would be Quanah.

Jael said, "I am willing to contact Josh Rivers, but it is very likely he is in Santa Fe now."

"You will go there and find him. I will send Growling Bear and Scratching Turkey with you for as far as it is safe for them. Your skill with the languages will see you the remainder of the way. Also, you may take the Rivers woman with you. She can do us no harm now, and she can help you find her brother."

"I will go, of course. But I must decide how to do this. When do you wish me to leave?"

"In two sunrises." He hesitated. "There is something else about which we must talk."

She looked at him questioningly. "Yes?"

"I have gathered certain things that the whites treasure and appear to use in trade."

"Like the gold nuggets you have used to pay Josh Rivers?"

"Yes, I have many more of those. I also have many gold pieces that have been removed from our dead enemies. No warriors were interested in these things, so I claimed these as my bounty."

"Money," she said in English, knowing no Comanche word for it.

"If I have these things when we surrender, they will be taken from me. Do you trust Rivers?"

"With the gold and coins, but not with my son."

"I cannot help you with your son. That will be your burden alone. I want you to take the gold and what you call 'money' to Rivers to hold for our people."

"I will do this."

9

"I AM NOT returning to Santa Fe," Tabitha said firmly.

"But you have no idea what winter will bring here. Food is already in short supply in the village. You have not lived a winter in a tipi. This is only the beginning of a dismal trail for the People. You should leave while you have the opportunity," Jael said.

"You will be gone for two, three, four weeks. Who knows how long this will take? Who will look after Flying Crow?"

"He can stay in Quanah's lodge. He has done so before when I have been sent on missions. Quanah's wives care for him as their own, and Quanah treats him as a son."

"I wouldn't want to face Josh after deserting his son. He is my nephew, and I will not leave him. Besides, my story is here. You said this was going be a dismal trail.

That sounds like a title for my book . . . 'Dismal Trail' . . . I need to be here if I'm going to have an ending for my story."

"You are as stubborn as your brother."

"Persistent. That's what Pop always calls it. A family trait."

"Then you are going to have to tell me how I find my way to your brother in Santa Fe."

"You go to his office on the Plaza, but first you go to a house I share with Danna, his law partner, and change into some of my clothes. We have a small stable next to the house where you can leave your horse. And that's something we must discuss."

"I am having difficulty following you. Are we discussing the house or the horse?"

"The horse. I want you to take my horse, Smokey, from the remuda and ride him to Santa Fe . . . and then leave him there. Josh will find you another. I do not want Smokey shot by soldiers or eaten by Comanche."

"I suppose I can do that. I believe Quanah claimed him."

"Then tell him to give him up. He's my horse."

"I will need to be more diplomatic than you suggest, but I will try."

"And I want you to take some articles for my newspaper. The *New Mexican* may be able to unwittingly help us."

"I am uncertain whether I should be a courier for your stories."

"Quanah is willing to let me return to Santa Fe. I would have delivered them myself and written many more. You can read the articles yourself, and if you find any of them harmful to the Kwahadi band, you may discard them. I think what I will be writing will soften the public when folks read the Comanche side of things. I will eventually write about both sides, but for a short time I will prostitute myself and try to do some public relations work for the Comanche. The horse killing story. I'll bet there's been nothing published about it in the American press, and it is a narrative that needs to be in print. Do you think Quanah can put me in touch with the warrior who brought him the news? I will need you to interpret, of course."

She could tell that Tabitha's mind was made up. She decided she should focus on organizing her journey today and tomorrow learn from her friend all she could about Santa Fe. She must speak to Quanah about Tabitha's horse and the plans for carrying out the proposed surrender. She was confident the ambitious chief had already worked out the scenario in his head.

10

THEY HAD BEEN on the trail for nearly a week, and Growling Bear and Scratching Turkey were showing signs of edginess as they picked up more signs of human activity. Tabitha had assured Jael that New Mexico and Santa Fe were teeming with every sort of Indian, and that they should trigger no suspicion unless they encountered someone with an unusually educated eye. Still, the diminutive Scratching Turkey and the other warrior, who looked his name, would not share a language with anyone they might meet, and there was unnecessary risk in having them accompany her further.

Scratching Turkey had just returned from scouting the area to the northwest and reported that a major trail leading westward lay directly ahead. He was certain it led to Santa Fe, and from a hilltop he could make out a city in the distance. It was early morning, and Jael decided it was a good time to part ways with her protectors. She pointed to a butte some distance to the south that rose from the earth like the watchtower of a castle and told the warriors they would rendezvous there, and if she did not come back within four sunsets, they should return to the village.

Jael grew increasingly anxious after parting with her friends. She had sent her bow and quiver with Growling Bear, fearing she might attract too much attention bearing the weaponry. She wished now she had brought the Henry rifle Tabitha had been teaching her to fire. She carried only a skinning knife in a sheath stitched to the inside of the thick buffalo hide vest she wore over her deerskin shirt. The well-worn shirt hung loosely over the denim trousers Tabitha had worn at the time of her capture. She supposed many would not recognize her as a woman had her hair not been tied back in Tabitha's favored pony tail. Without the braids, her friend had conjectured Jael's race was indefinable and that her lightly bronzed skin would allow her to pass for Indian, Mexican, or white, as she might need or choose.

She quickly came to the trail Scratching Turkey had discovered and reined Smokey west. No more than fifteen minutes later she spotted two riders riding up the rutted road toward her, moving their horses at a slow gallop. When they evidently sighted Jael, the men slowed their horses noticeably, and, as she approached, one rider swung his horse around to block her passage. She reined in Smokey, saying nothing as she studied the men. Both were slender men, one with a scraggly beard and grin revealing a gap where his two front teeth had been. The other was grim-faced with several days' growth of whiskers. They stunk of alcohol, the smell of which always angered her because of what the drink did to her tribesmen for several days after the Comancheros visited her village and made their trades.

The men sidled their horses up on each side of hers, trying to lock her mount between them. "Now ain't this a surprise?" the bearded man said. "I think we come upon a pretty little filly out on this road all by her lonesome." He reached out and placed a hand on her thigh. "You speakie English, little lady?"

She glanced at the other man, whose eyes were surveying her body. The hunger she saw there left no doubt about his intentions. The bearded man tightened his grip on her thigh, and the other leaned forward to grab her arm, but not before she had her skinning knife in her hand and swept it across the bridge of his nose, slicing deeply, leaving a chunk of flesh hanging from his face and blood spewing through the fingers that had instinctively clutched his wound.

The bearded man froze momentarily in shock, giving her time to whip the razor-sharp blade across his knuckles, dropping two fingers to the roadway. She tapped Smokey's flanks sharply with the heels of her moccasin-clad feet. He shot forward and raced down the dusty road, and Jael did not look back, the screams and sobs of her would-be attackers assuring her they would not be giving chase.

When she arrived on the outskirts of Santa Fe, Jael tried to recall Tabitha's directions about the location of the residence. Before she identified the landmarks, however, Smokey tossed his head and headed down a dusty side street. He acted as if he had a destination in mind, so she loosened her hold on the reins and let the gelding take the lead. Moments later, Smokey left the road and walked up a short trail that led to a small stable some twenty-five feet north of what appeared to be a solidly-constructed and well-maintained adobe house. The place matched Tabitha's description of her home perfectly, so Jael dismounted and led Smokey into the stable. She unsaddled the horse and removed the heavy saddlebags, and the animal walked directly to an empty stall. A sorrel mare in an adjacent stall whinnied a greeting, and from Smokey's reply, Jael gathered the horses were old friends. She caught sight of a stack of hay with a pitchfork sticking out from it in the corner of barn, and fed Smokey, dropping a token feeding in the neighbor's stall. Then she retrieved several buckets from pegs on the wall and pumped some water from the pump near the house's front entrance. She poured water in the metal trough that ran across a portion of the wall and through the stable partition, affording a water supply to the horses on both sides. Her chores completed, she stashed the saddlebags under the hay pile, and headed with her skinny bedroll for the back door of the house. She found a spare key, as Tabitha had promised, behind a loose adobe brick hidden by dry grass at the foundation's base and quickly entered the house.

She found the recessed closet in Tabitha's bedroom, crammed with a wardrobe that ran the gamut from striking gowns to tattered doeskin shirts and well-worn denim britches. The small chest next to the closet must be where the undergarments and other accessories were kept, Jael figured. It had been many years since she had worn such things, but Tabitha had insisted she would command more respect if she made her visit to this place called "the Plaza" attired as someone of importance.

First, she needed to wash off the trail dust and sweat accumulated from many days' riding. Tabitha had told her she would find a Mexican copper tub in a bathing closet off the kitchen. Jael entered the kitchen and pulled back a curtain to find an ornate claw-footed tub, which Tabitha had said was a luxury the house occupants had agreed they could not afford but had to have. Tabitha had insisted Jael start a fire in the wood stove and heat some water and soak in a hot bath. She vaguely remembered warm tub baths, but that was a luxury she no longer required, and she was in a hurry. She found a bucket and made herself a bath of ice-cold well water.

11

JAEL ENTERED THE law offices of Rivers and Sinclair, carrying the shoes she had worn for less than a quarter of the mile walk from the house Tabitha Rivers and Danna Sinclair shared. She sat down in one of the waiting room chairs, brushed off the soles of her stockings, squeezed her feet into the shoes and began lacing. She and Tabitha were a near perfect match for clothing sizes, but Jael had learned that her feet were uncomfortably larger than her friend's.

The waiting area was empty and she was uncertain what to do. She was ill at ease and felt clumsy in this environment. She had selected a dove-gray dress from the closet, although she was more naturally drawn to the burgundy and jade dresses there. For some reason, she recalled now that her mother had always had preferences for bright-colored clothing and likely would have called

Jael's current attire frumpy. It was strange how this venture into the small city had triggered memories from her life before the People.

She was startled momentarily when a petite, young Mexican woman, who had apparently been watching her from a hallway, spoke. "I'm sorry. I was in the library and didn't hear you come in. Please forgive me. I am Linda de la Cruz. May I help you?"

Jael stood up, wincing as her shoes pinched her sore toes. "I am Jael Chernik. I am here to see Mr. Rivers."

"He is attending a meeting at the courthouse. He should return in an hour or so. Is there something I can help you with?"

"Thank you, but I think not. May I wait here?"

"Of course. Miss Sinclair is available. Could she help you?"

Jael hesitated. "Perhaps I should meet her. You may tell her that I bring word from Quanah."

The young woman's eyes widened. "I knew your name was familiar. You are the one who is known as She Who Speaks. Josh has spoken of you many times. I know Danna would want to meet you. Wait just a moment." The young clerk scurried away and returned in a few minutes with a very tall, fair skinned woman, who had long, strawberry blonde hair and sapphire-blue eyes that Jael felt were searching into the very depths of her soul. The woman's smile seemed genuine and welcoming despite the appraising eyes, and Jael did not flinch at the young lawyer's scrutiny.

Danna Sinclair, after only a moment's hesitation, moved toward Jael and extended her hand. Jael received it with some confusion, for the practice of hand-shaking was foreign to her after so many years among the Comanche. Danna's grip was firm but brief, however, and Jael decided she did not find the experience the least unpleasant—just strange.

Danna said, "I've heard so much about you, but Josh's description of you . . . which you would find flattering . . . didn't do you justice. You are an incredibly striking woman."

Jael felt her cheeks flush and found herself uncomfortable with the compliment. "Thank you."

Danna took her by the arm. "Come back to my office. We can talk while you wait for Josh."

Danna led Jael into a small office with a window that opened onto the Plaza. A crackling fire in the small adobe-brick fireplace on the opposite wall banished the fall chill. Both women sat down in the captain's chairs that were positioned in front of the sturdy oak desk behind which Danna ordinarily sat. Jael suspected the seating choice signaled Danna's choice to assure Quanah's emissary of their positions as equals, a gesture she filed in her mind.

She cast her eyes about the room, noting the tall barrister bookcases and the framed diplomas and licenses adorning the walls. The room was tidy and might have seemed austere if not for the enormous woven, colorful Navajo rug that covered much of the floor. The expansive desktop, in contrast, was so cluttered with open books and scattered parchment sheets, that its surface was visible only at the edges.

Danna smiled and spoke, "Excuse the mess. I'm fairly organized about most things, but you wouldn't know it from my desk. I'm working on a case for a rancher challenging a portion of an old Spanish land grant. Boring to most lawyers. Fascinating to me."

"Mr. Rivers told me you are the only woman admitted to practice law in the territory."

"For the moment. There will be others. I may not live long enough to see it. But someday women will dominate the profession. That brings me to another thought. Josh says you have been, for all practical purposes, acting as Quanah's lawyer for some time now."

"I had never thought of it that way, and I am not entirely clear as to what lawyers do, but he does seek my opinion on some matters. My views are usually only solicited regarding concerns about dealing with the whites. Primarily he uses me as an interpreter, though."

"Josh and I have spoken about something that may interest you. We think Quanah and other bands and tribes will have a continuing need for lawyers to help them. We have decided to open an office near the reservation. You would be the perfect person to manage such an office. This idea has some selfish motivations on our part. Your management of the office would probably assure we would continue to receive Quanah's legal business. If you wanted, you could commence the study of law as a clerk under our firm's supervision and eventually take the bar examination and become a full member of the firm . . . and the second woman member of the territorial bar."

The proposal struck Jael like a bolt of lightning, and she had difficulty grasping the proposed scenario. "I cannot believe you are serious about this."

"I am very serious about this. At first, I was skeptical about Josh's idea to open an office near the reservation, but after thinking about it, I decided it made good sense. After meeting you, I am certain of it."

"I had not given much thought about what I would do after the war. I assumed I would remain with the People."

"I doubt if that would be permitted once the authorities learned you were a white captive. At least, that is the way the military would see it. You are a white captive to be repatriated."

"I do not think of myself as a captive."

"People with power may not care how you think of yourself. Regardless, you must realize that Michael will be removed from the Comanche and returned to his father."

"That will not happen."

"But it will. I'm sorry, but I do not do you any favor by not speaking frankly. Perhaps, if you make a place for yourself in the white world, you will be able to maintain contact with Michael."

Jael knew that the lawyer did not deserve her hostility, but she could not restrain her anger. "Your proposal begins to have the appearance of a bribe. This boy you call 'Michael' is Flying Crow. He is a Comanche, a member of the Kwahadi band. I am his mother, and he will remain with me."

"I do not mean to offend you. You would be perfect for the position, and it would be an opportunity for you. You do not have to decide now. And as for the future of Michael . . . Flying Crow . . . that is for you and Josh to resolve."

Jael did not wish to pursue the subject. She liked this woman and felt she could trust her with most things, but she was not about to share her plans for Flying Crow's future. There was no point, and it was likely Danna's first loyalty would be to her law partner. She had not quite worked out the details in her mind yet anyway.

Jael said, "I have spent a good amount of time discussing with Quanah the plans for taking the trail to the reservation. The past few months I have been tutoring him in the English language."

Danna furrowed her brow. "Really?"

"Yes. He is preparing for the inevitable in many ways. That is why I came to Santa Fe. Quanah knows the end is near. He still must convince some of the chiefs, but he sent me to urge Mr. Rivers to expedite negotiations. He seeks assurances from Colonel Mackenzie before he leads the People to the reservation. The People will be near starvation this winter. Mackenzie's soldiers are killing our horses and cutting off food supplies."

"I had heard rumors, but I thought they were probably just that: rumors."

"I have newspaper dispatches Tabitha Rivers sent with me that tells much of what is happening. She says that the truth will reveal a side of the Comanche that may bring some support to the plight of the People."

"Do you wish me to deliver the dispatches to the *New Mexican*?"

"That would be kind of you. They are in your home."

"My home?"

"Tabitha's horse, Smokey, is in your stable. She feared he would be slaughtered for meat when the winter food supplies disappeared. I will need to locate another horse for my return to the village."

"I can take care of that." She hesitated. "I thought your dress was familiar. It's Tabby's, isn't it?"

"Yes. I confess that I invaded your home. Tabitha told me where to find a key, and I bathed and changed into her clothing there. I drew some stares when I came into the Plaza carrying my shoes, however. My feet are somewhat larger than hers."

"You will spend the night at our house . . . and as many nights as you wish. This evening you will dine with me at La Castillo. When we are finished here, Linda will take you to Spiegelberg's Mercantile and help you find a pair of shoes that fit."

"I have no money with me."

"We have funds of Quanah's in the firm trust account. He can purchase your shoes."

Jael was uncomfortable with the thought of dining in public. She had done so on occasion in New York and

Berlin, but that seemed so long ago. Yet, not much more than eight years had passed since the Chernik family departed New York. How ironic that she had today arrived at the destination where Tevel Chernik had planned to set up his medical practice before the Comanche war party intervened. She had reached her fourteenth birthday on the trail, and, unlike many younger white captives, had vivid memories of another life, memories that had slept for some years now, and were awakening with this venture into the so-called civilized world. She found herself confused and disconcerted at the intrusion of the recollections.

A rapping on the office door startled Jael.

12

JOSH WALKED INTO Danna's office to find Danna and Jael seated in the clients' chairs at the front of the desk. Danna immediately got up and nodded to Josh to take her place, while she moved behind the desk to her usual swivel chair.

"Hello, Joshua," Jael said.

"Jael. I didn't expect to find you here. At least not until Linda told me Danna was speaking with a young lady from Quanah's village." He sat down and searched her dark eyes for a moment. She returned his gaze, and he could read nothing there.

"Quanah sent me. I am to tell you he wants to negotiate peace. He will bring all the People who will join him to the reservation. By spring that will be most, if not all, I suspect. He wants you to go to Fort Sill and speak to the commandant or Indian agent . . . anyone who makes the final decisions . . . and get whatever commitments you can. He realizes he does not speak from a position of strength, but he still wants a promise of land and cattle and assurance that none of the Kwahadi chiefs will be imprisoned. He wants a promise that the horses will not be taken and killed. He asks that the tribal councils be heard on military and government decisions that affect the various bands. He also wants to unofficially, for now, be the designated spokesman for the Comanche nation. Finally, he will sign no treaty. His word must suffice."

"For a man who knows he speaks from weakness, he's making a lot of demands."

"He is a war chief. He is prepared to lead the Comanche in peace. He aspires to be the first chief of all Comanche. Our tribesmen on the reservation report Mackenzie is going to be appointed the next commanding officer there. Convince him that Quanah has the skills and influence to make Colonel Mackenzie's tenure at Fort Sill much more effective."

"You can be a part of that, too. Did Danna speak with you about working for our firm?"

"We discussed your proposal. I cannot answer now. I have a son who stands in the way of my answer. I do not trust you on that question. I must know your intentions."

Josh bristled. "I also have a son. And I do not trust you on that question. But I will tell you this. He will be returned to his family, and he will live with me. But I will make some accommodation so you can visit him and be a part of his life."

Her eyes shot fire, and Josh knew he had not handled this well. But he spoke the truth, and he did not want to disillusion the woman, especially since he respected her so much.

Danna interceded. "This discussion leads up a dead-end canyon. I suggest we keep our conversation focused on Jael's mission to Santa Fe." She turned to Josh. "Can you speak with Mackenzie?"

"I will certainly try. I will ride to Fort Sill and approach Dr. Sturm. He has the contacts who should get me a hearing with the right people. I'll try to leave within a few weeks, if the weather holds. This deep into December, things can turn nasty overnight, but I have no choice but to complete some business here, since I will be gone a spell."

Danna said, "I would think you could get there and conduct your business and be back here in a few weeks."

"But I have to get the details of the peace agreement to Quanah. If terms are acceptable, I'll join Quanah on the trail to the reservation."

"It will be a dismal trail," Jael pronounced solemnly.

Josh could not argue the point with her. "I will need to know how to find you."

She was silent for some moments, as if pondering whether to trust him. "The village is located at the southernmost end of the canyon some whites call Palo Duro. The Kwahadi and remnants of other bands . . . and some Kiowa . . . are settled there for the winter. If you are near, you will be found. But you should be aware there are many who have no interest in your mission and would gladly kill you."

"That seems to be an occupational hazard. I will be there before spring."

"There is something else I must discuss with both of you," Jael said. "I brought gold with me."

"Gold?"

"Yes. Quanah sent his gold with me. I knew he had gold nuggets he gave me to pay your fees, but he had more gold than I could ever imagine hidden someplace. Gold means nothing to most Comanche, but I gather from trading with the Comanchero, Quanah determined the metal is valuable in the white man's world. He has gold coins, small nuggets, even rings and other jewelry . . . . collected from his dead enemies, I assume. His treasure fills the pockets of army saddlebags I brought with me. The gold is presently in a stack of hay in Danna's stable."

"In the stable? Do you realize you probably have a small fortune stashed in a barn where anyone could pick it up?" Josh asked, his tone scolding.

"And where else would I put it? I cannot imagine anyone would be looking for treasure in a horse barn. But I certainly agree it should be removed as soon as possible. Quanah was concerned the soldiers would confiscate the gold when he surrenders. He wants to use the gold to help his people establish a new life on the reservation. In the meantime, he asks that you secure its safety."

Danna said, "We have a large safe in the office that would hold the gold for now. I suggest selling, perhaps, a quarter of it and opening accounts at both the First National Bank and the Spiegelberg's Second National Bank for the funds, so we don't have all the eggs in a single basket. That way, Quanah will have immediate funds to draw on."

Josh interrupted, "We cannot put Quanah's name on a bank account."

"No," Danna replied, "of course not. But, for now, we could open it in the name of 'Comanche Land & Cattle Company' and designate you and Jael as signatories. The bank papers could require two signatures for a draft.

Someday the account would be turned over to Quanah. You and Jael could take care of signing at the banks in the morning. I'll handle filing incorporation papers at the courthouse tomorrow. Temporarily, the public record will show members of our firm as officers and directors. What do you think, Jael?"

"I do not understand this, but I am confident Quanah would tell me to follow your advice."

Josh said, "Danna, I'll ride over to your house and find the gold and bring it back and put it in the safe for now."

Jael said, "I can remain tomorrow to take care of any business matters, but I must leave the next morning. I am to meet Growling Bear and Scratching Turkey soon."

"I had assumed some warriors came with you. I hope they haven't tried to collect some scalps east of Santa Fe."

"Why do you say that?"

"While I was at the federal courthouse, somebody reported to the U. S. Marshall that two men were attacked by a band of Indians on the trail east. One gentleman had part of his nose sliced off and the other lost a couple of fingers. Strange injuries."

"I assure you, Joshua, if a band of Comanche got close enough to inflict those wounds, the gentlemen would not have escaped with either their scalps or their lives."

Josh studied Jael's face with a suspicion she was not telling him all she knew about the story. "I suppose that's true enough."

Danna said, "Josh, why don't you retrieve the gold while I introduce Jael to Marty and Tara." She turned to Jael and explained, "Martin Locke is the newest member of our firm, and Tara Hemphill is our other clerk. You should get acquainted with everyone in case you decide to accept our offer."

"And we hope you will," Josh added.

"Josh, Linda's taking Jael shopping, and then Jael and I intend to have dinner this evening. Tomorrow morning, Jael will meet you here at the office at nine-thirty sharp. You can discuss any more details about the peace negotiations and take care of the banking arrangements."

"I could join you for dinner tonight."

"But you're not invited. If you treat Jael well, perhaps, she would consider dining with you tomorrow evening."

13

THE FLICKERING CANDLESTICK in the simple sconce attached to the plastered adobe wall adjacent to their table cast a shimmering glow on Jael's flawless skin, and Josh decided he had never dined with a more beautiful woman. She wore a burgundy gown that scooped below her shoulders just enough to reveal a hint of cleavage below the silver pendant that dropped from her swanlike neck. Her sable hair, tied back with a ribbon that matched her dress, swept like a waterfall over her shoulders. Danna's work, he suspected.

Admittedly, he had found her stunning in buckskins and moccasins, but it was different somehow. She was of another world then, a world in which he did not belong. She must be looking with trepidation to the months that lay ahead, moving from a culture she had made her own and returning to a society that had nurtured her through childhood. Now, with the passage of years, he supposed she was finding herself neither Comanche nor white. And then there was this issue that stood like a mighty wall between them: Michael.

It suddenly occurred to him that they had barely spoken since leaving the buggy he had rented for the evening and that there had been total silence between them since they were seated. She seemed absorbed in studying the menu lying on the table in front of her. "I'm sorry," he said. "I haven't been very attentive."

"Sometimes, silence is a good thing between people."

"Do you find anything of interest on the menu?"

"I was just looking at the offerings. Everything is printed in both English and Spanish, and I realized that I speak Spanish with some fluency, but I can read very little of it. This is something I must remedy."

Josh smiled at her seriousness. "I have no doubt you will. I understand many scholars learn to read and write the language but can never master the art of conversing comfortably. You have a head start."

A Mexican waiter appeared with two wine glasses and a bottle of red wine. He set the glasses on the table and filled them nearly full and asked if they were ready to order. Josh looked at Jael. "American or Mexican?"

"American. I had something called burritos and refried beans at La Castillo last night. It was very good, but I think I would prefer something else tonight."

"Your American choices tonight appear to be steak or steak."

She smiled. He could not recall seeing her smile before, but it was radiant and warming. "I believe I will have the steak."

Josh ordered steak and fried potatoes with cherry cobbler for dessert for both. "Are you still leaving in the morning?" he asked.

"Yes. I must."

"I could ride with you until you meet Growling Bear and Scratching Turkey. There are some unsavory characters riding in and out of Sant Fe."

"I will be fine. Danna gave me a gun called an Army Colt and taught me to use it this afternoon."

"That might do for one man, but if you run into a bunch of renegades, you might just as well try fighting them off by throwing pebbles."

"Please, I can take care of myself."

He chose not to press the issue, but decided he would be at Danna's before sunrise, anyway. He changed the subject. "Well, what do you think of Santa Fe now that you've seen the sights?"

"It is like going to a circus . . . I remember such things from Germany and New York. There is so much to see, the pueblos on the outskirts, the huge mercantile and the mixing of peoples is so interesting. Even German Jews, like I once was. Or am. I am not certain. I have yet to sort that out."

"Willi Spiegelberg was nearly speechless when you spoke to him in German. I couldn't understand a word once the two of you started conversing in his native tongue. I swear he fell in love with you and would have signed over the bank if you asked."

"I have had little opportunity to speak the language for some years, but it came back quickly. Of course, German was my first language, and I often think in German to this day. That seems strange, doesn't it . . . thinking in a language?"

They spoke about everything but the verboten subject—Michael—as they ate, and he delighted in hearing about her childhood and some of the humorous stories about Comanche life. Josh found himself sharing stories about his family and his accidental journey to becoming a law wrangler. Just as they finished their cobbler, Josh heard a familiar voice.

"Josh, you must introduce me to your lady." Oh, God. It was Jessica.

Josh stood and turned, as Jessica rushed up and brushed her lips against his cheek and gave him a quick hug, before turning her scrutiny to Jael. The young Comanche woman met Jessica's eyes evenly, he noted, her face showing more curiosity than discomfort. "This is my business associate, Jael Chernik," Josh said. "Jael, this is Jessica Chandler, manager and director of the Teatro Santa Fe, our local theatre and arts center . . . and a good friend of mine."

Jessica extended her hand, and Jael, remaining seated, received it, each woman seemingly fixing her eyes on the other's face. Finally, Jessica stepped back and said. "I just know I've seen you someplace before. Have we met? Back east, perhaps?"

"Have you performed in Berlin?" Jael answered evasively.

"Never. Oh, my God. I do know you. I saw you in the Comanche camp. You are the interpreter, She Who Speaks."

"Jess," Josh said softly. "Lower your voice, please."

"I don't understand. I would have bet two gold eagles this was the woman who—"

"Jessica, this is Jael Chernik. We are business associates. Nothing else. You have mistaken her for someone else. Trust me."

"I know who she is. But I'll keep your little secret if you'll promise to tell me the story someday."

"I promise."

"But, now I know she's the other woman in our bed . . . I mean the room." Seemingly unflustered, Jessica said, "So nice to meet you, Miss Chernik. I will talk with you soon, Josh. Good evening." With those words, Jessica Chandler vanished as quickly as she had appeared.

Josh sat down at the table, speechless after Jessica's whirlwind visit.

Jael broke the silence. "I know that woman. She was with you the morning of your capture by Quanah's war party. You were sharing her robe, I heard." Her lips were closed, but they formed the faint traces of an impish smile.

"Jessica is a good friend," he replied. "Most of the time."

14

A CHILL HAD WAFTED down from the mountains and settled on Santa Fe by the time Josh gently tugged the horse's reins and pulled the buggy to a stop in front of Danna's house. He helped Jael out of the buggy, knowing she would do fine without his assistance and obviously felt awkward receiving it.

"I had a nice evening," he said, as he walked her to the door, feeling clumsy as a fifteen-year-old boy.

"It was enjoyable. Thank you for an interesting evening. My visit to Santa Fe has been an experience I shall not soon forget."

He was uncertain how to take her words. He stopped in front of the door and gently pulled her to him and wrapped his arms around her. He felt her body stiffen as he lowered his head. Their lips touched softly, then lingered, before she relaxed and leaned into him for a moment before suddenly pulling away. His last glimpse of her eyes before she turned and rushed into the house revealed the panic of a cornered animal, and those dark eyes would haunt him in the days and months ahead.

He returned before sunrise the next morning, but Danna informed him that Jael had ridden out during the night. "She was obviously upset about something," Danna said. "Did you quarrel about Michael?"

"No," Josh replied. "But he was with us."

15

A RAW, RELENTLESS WIND swept across the Staked Plains as Jael and her warrior escorts descended into the canyon and escaped some of the frigid blasts. The air felt heavy and damp, and Jael was certain a snowstorm was trailing them. The trek from Santa Fe had taken the better part of two weeks because of detours forced by the need to avoid patrolling soldiers. She took a deep breath as a surge of relief came when she caught sight of the seemingly endless columns of swirling smoke rising from the canyon floor. Their pace seemed snaillike, however, as their sure-footed mounts picked their ways down the narrow trail.

She was impatient and excited to see Flying Crow when they reached the village, but she knew her duty and went directly to Quanah's lodge. The young war chief stood in front of the tipi, obviously expecting her.

She supposed he had been forewarned by one of the sentries of her journey down the trail that edged the canyon wall. He signaled for her to follow him into the tipi. She stepped into the tipi, and the heat from the fire embraced her, and she relaxed for the first time since they headed out for Santa Fe. She was safe and warm in the womb of the lodge. She had returned to Flying Crow and the People. She was home.

After they were seated on buffalo robes near the fire, Quanah spoke in Comanche. "I expected you seven sunrises ago. I feared the white eyes had captured or killed you."

"The pony soldiers have many patrols six sunrises north. We had to change our course many times to avoid them."

Quanah nodded. "They will find us when the grass grows again. We have been able to run and hide many times, but the cougar's jaw is slowly closing and will soon catch us in its teeth. Even Isa-Tai is losing faith in our ability to resist. The other chiefs are surrendering to the truth of what is coming. We must go to the reservation and make the best of it and learn the white man's ways."

It was not her place to express an opinion, so she simply replied. "You are a wise man. You will decide what is best for the People and lead them on the proper path."

"My decision has been made, and I believe most will follow. Tell me, what does our man Rivers say? Will he see Bad Hand Mackenzie?"

"He will try. He will travel to Fort Sill soon. He will seek the best terms he can for the Kwahadi band and our allies. He cannot promise the white chiefs will agree to all you have asked. Even if they do, I do not think he trusts his own people very much."

"Then he is the wise man I believed him to be. Do you still trust him?"

She thought for a moment before answering. "You can trust him."

"But some cannot?"

"He is an honorable man in most matters. But Flying Crow grew from his seed. He insists he must be returned. He will do anything to make that happen. And I would not trust him not to take my son by any means he deems necessary. I have said as much before."

"The soldiers will not allow you to keep him when they learn. They will take you away from the People also. I am saddened by this. Other mothers are grieving, for they know that their adopted children will be torn from their families and given to strangers."

"I can do something about this. I have memories of the white world. I speak the language of the white eyes. I will leave the village before the soldiers come, and I will take my son to a place where they cannot find us."

Quanah got up and moved to the tipi's edge, where he knelt and slipped his hand under a small stack of skins. He plucked out a small deerskin bag and returned and handed it to her. "I did not send all of my gold with you. I kept this and two other bags, which I can hide and keep with me. You have been my loyal counselor. This bag has the gold that white eyes use for trade. It will help you make a new place." With a glum look on his face, he declared. "Our freedom will fly away with the eagle soon. You may have your son, but I fear you will never know the freedom the People know now."

16

THE WIND HOWLED like a pack of wolves as it whipped through the canyon and drove violent blasts against the tipi. The tipi walls trembled, but Jael was confident they would hold, and the wood supply would last for several days, if necessary. Their buffalo robes would keep them warm and cozy.

Flying Crow had chattered like a chipmunk for most of the evening, stopping only intermittently to listen with awe to his mother's tales of the strange things she had seen in Santa Fe. Tonight, it struck her for the first time just how foreign this new world that was almost upon them would be to him. He had suddenly dropped off to sleep just minutes earlier, and she treasured his closeness now, as his head rested on her lap.

Flying Crow had so dominated her time, since she opened the lodge flap and entered shortly before dusk, that she had spoken no more than a few words to Tabitha Rivers, who faced her from the other side of the sputtering fire. "I think he has finally surrendered for the night," Jael said softly.

"He was thrilled to have you back. He's been asking about you every day. He's a bit of a worrier."

"Yes. Unfortunately, he has greater worries ahead." She changed the subject. "Your brother sends his love. He said to tell you he still thinks you are insane."

Tabitha smiled. "Insanity is in our blood. Mostly Pop's fault, I think. That's what Mom used to say. She always blamed Pop for any craziness the boys and I got into. And I don't think she was jesting."

Jael envied Tabitha her family bond. From her friend's talk over their months together, Jael had concluded the Rivers siblings were a close-knit bunch even when miles separated. Knowing this, she struggled to decide how honest to be with Tabitha about what she planned. She determined that silence was the best course. Still, she wanted to fish for information about Joshua Rivers and his mindset. "Your brother and I quarreled about Flying Crow's future after the Comanche travel to Fort Sill."

She could see the concern in Tabitha's dark eyes. "I'm sorry." Tabitha said. "Did you decide anything?"

"He decided Flying Crow would be taken from me and go to live with him. I decided that would not happen."

"Jael, you are the only mother Michael has ever known. And you have been a good mother. But you must reach some compromise."

"You call him Michael now," Jael said coldly.

"Yes, I taught him to print his name while you were in Santa Fe, and he is learning to read words and sentences. He is very bright. Because you started teaching him so early, he speaks English without an accent. He is well prepared for the changes that are coming to his life. I felt it was time for him to become accustomed to his name."

"I suppose that is true, but his friends among the People will not change their way of calling him."

"That is fine, but surely you realize he will not be living with the Comanche. Josh is a lawyer, and he will demand that the Army remove him from the tribe. I'm sorry, Jael. You are like a sister to me, and it pains me to see you hurt. But you must prepare for this."

"I am preparing."

"There is no kinder and fairer person than Josh. He will find ways for you to remain in touch with Michael. You will remain a part of his life."

"A part of his life. Yes, I suppose. That is what Joshua says, too. And I agree, he must become accustomed to his new name." She spoke without emotion. Her words were as dead as she felt at this moment.

Jael gently lifted the boy's head from her lap and slipped him under his buffalo robe, which lay near the fire. She got up and retrieved her own robe and placed it next to his. Silently, she plucked a few oak logs from the stack along the inner wall near the tipi's entrance and placed them on the fire, taking care not to scatter sparks. Then she crawled under her own robe, leaving Tabitha sitting in front of the fire.

"We need to discuss this," Tabitha said.

Jael did not reply.

"You're not going to talk about Michael, are you?"

Jael said, "No."

Cocooned in the warm robe, Jael's mind raced, belying the calm facade she had displayed to Tabitha. She was caught in a whirlpool of emotions. Her visit to Santa Fe had verified she could make her way again in the so-called civilized world. The opportunity Danna Sinclair had offered sounded interesting and exciting. She regretted she would be unable to accept it. Josh's kiss. It had sent a ripple of desire through her body that was unfamiliar to her. And it frightened her. She knew it was a part of his strategy to tear down her defenses before he absconded with her son. He was shrewd, and he would never, never stop his quest. And she would not give up her son. It was much later, after seemingly endless mulling over different alternatives for her escape, that Jael fell asleep.

17

OSH'S JOURNEY TO Fort Sill had been delayed by winter storms that hammered Santa Fe off and on for the better part of two weeks. No one could recall seeing snow piled a foot deep on the Plaza before. Well, they'd better take a quick look, he thought, because a false spring had dropped on the town just as suddenly as the icy blasts had hit a few weeks earlier. It was mid-January, but the air was balmy and the snow was quickly disappearing into slush and mud.

Josh tried to keep to the narrow boardwalk as he headed for the Teatro Santa Fe where he expected to find Jessica. They had not spoken since the evening she stopped by the table when he and Jael were dining at the Exchange. While he had been banished from her bed, they were still good friends, and he was one of the investors in the forum that was trying to bring culture to Santa Fe.

When he reached the theatre, he lifted the latch on the Navajo-carved double doors and pushed. The doors did not give. That meant they were bolted from the inside. Since there was no padlock on the outside, that meant Jessica must be in the building, evidently not wanting to be interrupted by social callers or curiosity-seekers.

She was no doubt engaged in a decorating or renovation project. He tapped on the door, but she did not respond. He decided she must be in the theatre proper and could not hear him, so he pounded heavily on the solid door and waited. Soon, he heard the snap of the iron deadbolt, and the door inched open. Jessica's dark eyes peeked out through the space between the open doors.

"Josh," she said, "what are you doing here?"

"Nice to see you, too," he replied.

She opened the door and gestured for him to enter. "I just meant your visit is a surprise. I'm always glad to see you."

He noticed her voice did not project any enthusiasm for his appearance. Normally, he would have been greeted with a hug and kiss, perhaps, a more provocative brush of her fingers if she was in the mood, which was about always. Also, she was usually immaculate and well-kempt, even when painting a wall or hammering a nail.

This afternoon, her hair was uncharacteristically disheveled, and the top button of her blouse was not fastened.

She closed the door, and led him into the former church building's expansive foyer. "There is someone here you must meet. Oliver," she called, "could you come up? I have a dear friend I would like you to meet."

A few moments later, a dark-complexioned man standing a bit under six feet, appeared in the doorway of the performance area. He wore a checkered cotton shirt that struggled to contain his muscular arms and shoulders, and the new denim trousers were equally stretched against bulging thighs. Josh had no doubt that Jessica had seen and caressed the firm, muscular flesh the garments covered. He felt a twinge of jealousy, knowing he had no right.

Josh strolled across the room and extended his hand. "We've met. Oliver Wolf, isn't it?"

"Yes, Mr. Rivers," Wolf said, taking Josh's hand in a firm grip, "under less pleasant circumstances. I planned to call on you soon to inquire whether you had any news of your sister."

"I cannot confirm how I know this, but I have every reason to believe she is safe and well. But she is still with the Comanche. When we last met, you were scouting for Mackenzie."

"My contract was up, and after the slaughter of the horses, I wanted no more to do with the Red River War."

"Tabby wrote of this in a dispatch she was able to deliver to the *New Mexican* but all she could attest to were rumors."

"They were not rumors."

Jessica interrupted. "I'll be right back." She hurried away and returned with a large folder filled with parchment sheets. She placed the folder on the ticket counter and began removing the papers and spreading them out on the smooth oak counter top. "Josh, look at these. Oliver did these sketches. He is very talented."

Josh studied the drawings. Almost all included horses, several mounted by soldiers, others racing free and, finally, a depiction of the killing of the horses. Soldiers firing, horses stumbling and sinking to the earth, a canyon floor littered with equine corpses. The drawings brought tears to his eyes.

"And look at this one," Jessica said. She rolled out a sheet she had obviously been saving. It was a magnificent, muscled stallion standing near a stream, his head turned toward the artist. He appeared black or gray in color, but with the penciled drawing one could not be certain. But his eyes were enclosed within large, white, only slightly irregular circles, giving him a ghostly look.

Below the drawing was the word "Spared." Josh had never seen a drawing so captivating.

"Oliver. I know very little about art, but to me these are masterpieces. You are extremely talented. You could sell these for a good sum. I'm certain of it."

"They're not for sale. Not right now, anyway. I hope to use these sketches as my models for larger oil paintings, which I would expect to sell."

"The stallion . . . he was with the Comanche herds?"

"And he's mine now. I call him 'Owl.' The colonel allowed the scouts to each select two horses before the slaughter. I have a mouse-gray filly at the livery, also."

"What a waste. I don't understand it."

"It's a simple strategy. Horses are wealth to the Comanche. My Cherokee brothers value their horses as well, but they are not our life-blood. For the Comanche, the horse is not only his currency but his tool for survival. He depends on the horse to hunt buffalo and deer and to carry his robes and tipis as he moves from place to place. And engage in war without the horse? He is at the mercy of his enemies without the beast."

"It has really become a matter of starving out those who remain off the reservation, hasn't it?"

"And to assure they stay on the reservation when they arrive, the army is confiscating the horses and killing them."

The fools. Josh had to address this with Mackenzie. The fate of the horses had to be a part of any terms.

Jessica said, "Oliver just arrived in Santa Fe two weeks ago. New Year's Day to be precise. I was here cleaning up after the holiday concert and party, and he walked in looking for work. He is also a skilled carpenter, so I have employed him to design and build an expansion of the stage. He will work for half his usual rate in exchange for being allowed to display the art he produces in the foyer. He also sculpts. We'll sell his work and take a ten per cent commission. Do you think the board will approve?"

"I don't see why not. Jess, I stopped by to tell you I'm leaving town tomorrow. I may be gone for several months. I'll leave you my proxy to cast my vote on any matters that come before the board, but I can't imagine you'll have any problems. You're probably operating the only theatre outside New York that's returning a profit for its shareholders."

"You're never in town. I don't know how your partners put up with it. Where are you headed this time?"

"Fort Sill. That's all I can say."

Wolf spoke, "Mr. Rivers, I don't have any right to ask, but does any of this have to do with recovering your sister from the Comanche?"

"And my son, yes."

"I know the Staked Plains. I've done nothing but scout it for a year. I've spent time at Sill, too. I'd be honored to ride with you."

"Oliver, you can't do that," Jessica protested. "You just got here. You can't go off like this."

"I will return. I promise. I owe Tabitha Rivers my life. This is my chance to pay her back, with Mr. Rivers's permission."

"My client has funds available to hire your assistance, Oliver," Josh said. "And I'd welcome your company, if you will call me 'Josh.'"

Wolf smiled. "Josh, it is."

Jessica's lips pursed in a severe pout. "You son of a bitch, Josh Rivers. I hope you freeze your tiny balls off on your way to Fort Sill."

18

JOSH FOUND OLIVER Wolf a congenial companion. He was a well-spoken man, educated in a Quaker school near his Cherokee settlement in west Arkansas. While he carried more Cherokee blood than anything else, he had a Scottish grandfather and a mother who was part Tonkawa. He had no formal artistic training, although he had assisted a sculptor who was carving a granite civil war monument near his home. Wolf had served in the Confederate army as a major in the First Cherokee Brigade. Officers were often young men during that conflict, but Josh figured Wolf had to be older than he appeared, likely in his early thirties.

The balmy weather still held, so Josh decided to bypass the main trail and stop by his brother Cal's Circle M Ranch in northeastern New Mexico. He had not seen Cal's six-month-old since shortly after the boy's birth in

Santa Fe, an event Cal had missed because he was with Josh on an unsuccessful mission to recover Michael and Tabby from the Kwahadi. They had encountered Wolf and Charles Goodnight on that trek.

As they rode into the ranch yard, a huge gray and black-spotted dog of unidentifiable origins announced their arrival with a gruff barking and raced toward them. Suddenly, he pulled up short and bared his teeth, emitting a threatening growl. Josh's buckskin gelding ignored the animal, but Wolf's owl-eyed stallion danced nervously, and the mare packhorse fought her lead rope.

"We'll just wait," Josh said. "Somebody sure as hell heard him."

On cue, a voice called from the pine-planked barn. "Big brother, come on over to the barn. That cur's all bark. I guarantee he won't bite."

Josh and Wolf headed for the barn and hitched the horses to a corral fence. Josh noticed that the guard dog had evidently grown quickly bored and returned to wherever he was napping. The two men ambled into the barn through the wide door, and found Cal bloodied and shirtless in a stall at the far end, one arm half buried in a mare's womb. He stepped back, the mare strained several times, and a foal, slick with afterbirth, dropped on the straw-covered floor. Cal knelt to be sure its mouth was clear, looked under the foal's tail and then untied the mare before backing out of the stall and closing the gate. "A little girl," Cal said. "Mom probably would have been fine without my help, but I couldn't chance losing another foal. Lost three to the storm a few weeks back. Oh, by the way big brother, welcome to the Circle M, such as it is." He stepped toward Josh and swallowed him in a bear hug. Cal, standing at more than six feet four inches, was the tallest of the Rivers clan, lean and rangy, and strong enough to wrestle a bear Josh figured.

Then he turned to Wolf and offered his hand. "I should know you."

"Think Charles Goodnight," Josh said.

"I'll be damned. You're that guy Michael about killed with his spear. Would have if Goodnight hadn't found you. Wolf something, as I recall."

Wolf tendered a sheepish grin. "I go by Oliver Wolf these days. I didn't know the boy was Josh's son at the time, but I nearly got scalped trying to rescue a woman who didn't want to be rescued."

"Well, me and Josh didn't do any better. We left Quanah's camp with our tails between our legs and nothing to show for it. Tabby says she's got to stay with those devils and write a damn book. She's crazier than hell. Got it from Pop, I think." Cal had a contentious relationship with his father, given he had scorned the Slash R to scout for the Army, and was a reluctant cattleman at best.

Josh leaned up against a stall gate and asked, "How's Erin and the kids?"

"Well, little Willow's turning into a real beauty. Can't keep up with her. Jabbers a lot, but I can't understand much of what she says."

"She's not even three years old, Cal. You can't expect her to preach sermons yet."

"Don't need sermons. Get enough of that from her mom."

Willow was Erin's daughter by a Comanche warrior, conceived during captivity. Josh and Cal had ransomed Erin, and the baby had been born during their return from Quanah's village. It was then that Cal and the flame-haired Erin had formed a bond that led to their marriage a month before Zack was born.

"And Zack?"

"Rowdy kid. Eats good. Growing. Screams half the night. Erin brings him to bed to suckle. Don't get any sleep. Don't get anything else, if you know what I mean."

"I'm anxious to see them."

"Well, you're going to have to wait a spell. They ain't here."

"They're not?"

"They went to Pop's. I sent the German with them. Erin said she needed to get out of here. She decided to go visit her aunt Dawn."

The German was Hans Schmidt, a young immigrant who stood six and a half feet tall and had once been employed by Levi Rivers. He had joined Cal when he and Erin took over the ranch after her late father's death. He was a gentle giant and a hard worker. His English was rudimentary, and it occurred to Josh that Jael would likely enjoy refreshing her German language skills with the man. "You should have gone with her. Pop was in Santa Fe last week complaining he hadn't seen you since the wedding last summer."

"The old bastard knows the way here. We're a third the distance from his place as Santa Fe. Besides, Erin didn't want me to go along. She's pissed at me."

"Well, that doesn't surprise me. But you seemed to be the happiest couple in the state six months ago."

"And I thought we was. But not long after the little guy came along, she started having crying fits and being mopey most of the time in between. And she bitched at me all the time because the ranch is going broke and we never have any money."

"Most ranchers are land poor. We never had any money growing up, and Pop still carries a good-sized note at the bank."

"I know that. But I was never cut out for ranching. I like raising some horses, but there ain't any money in it. I like eating beef, but that's about all I care about as far as the damn cattle are concerned. Besides, this is Erin's ranch. I feel like a kept man here. And she's hinted at that a few times."

Josh was shocked at Cal's mental state. His younger brother was usually a happy-go-lucky sort, and very little perturbed him much. "I don't know what to say, Cal."

"I don't, either. I sure as hell don't." Then he gave a forced smile. "Hey, I'm not much of a host. It's getting on to supper time. Put up your horses and come up to the house. I'll try to cobble together some vittles and make us some supper. Got nobody else to feed. Laid off most of the hands . . . for winter anyway. Only two left, besides the German, and they are out at one of the line shacks tonight checking on the herd. They'll be back by noon tomorrow. I don't promise a fancy meal. I don't cook for shit."

"I know. I've ridden some trails with you."

After keeping quiet during the brothers' exchange, Wolf spoke. "I'll cook if you don't mind. I ran a chuck wagon for a season at a ranch a few years back."

Cal's face showed noticeable relief. "You just got yourself a job, friend."

"Oliver, is there anything you don't do?" Josh asked.

The usually somber man shrugged and surrendered a closed-lip smile. "Not much."

19

"YOU WANT A job as a cook, Oliver, you're sure welcome to stay on here. Of course, I can't pay you nothing," Cal said, as they finished supper at the kitchen table. Cal had scrounged up some beans and bacon and pointed Oliver to the flour and canned fruit, and the Cherokee had put two Dutch ovens and a skillet to work in the fireplace, choosing to ignore the new cookstove. The beans and bacon had been cooked in the skillet, and biscuits and apple cobbler had been produced from the ovens. Cal had handled the coffee, which wasn't bad if you had a cast iron stomach, Josh thought.

Cal already knew about Josh's relationship with Quanah, so Josh had filled him in on his plans. "I suppose we could be gone the better part of two months," Josh said. "But, Oliver, after I find Quanah, there would be no reason for you to stay."

"How about I come with you?"

"You can't do that. You've got a ranch to run."

"I don't run anything. At most I'm Erin's foreman. Right now, Branch Cambridge can look after things when he and Gimpy get in from the line shack tomorrow."

"But what happens when Erin gets home?"

"She'll be madder than a mama bear. Probably fire me."

"You're not leaving her and the kids?"

"Hell no, but me and Ham's got something going."

"You and Ham?" Josh could not imagine what Ham and Cal would be conspiring to do. Hamilton Rivers was a Denver banker and the second eldest of the Rivers brothers; Nate, who ramrodded the Slash R, being the first born.

"Yup. Ham's coming down from Denver in June to talk and work out the particulars of setting up a Denver to Santa Fe Freight company. He'll arrange the money and look after the financial end, but I'll hire the men, find the horses and wagons and run the day to day operations. He says I can even be the president of the damn thing. How's this sound? President Calvin Rivers."

Josh chuckled. "It does have an impressive ring to it."

"And once Erin gets over the fact I ain't talked this over with her, she'll like it fine. We get along better being apart from time to time. She can run this place the way she wants, and I'll have my own business to look after. But if this pays off the way Ham thinks it will, she'll be glad to spend the extra money the company brings in. Probably buy more of this godforsaken land and half-starved cows. We might fuss a bit over what to do with the freight profits."

"From what you say, I don't doubt it. I guess if you want to come along, you're welcome."

"As long as I don't do the cooking."

"I won't let you do the cooking. And I'll make the coffee."

20

THE THREE MEN followed the Canadian River east from Cal's, and, after a few days, cut south to the Red River, which they planned to keep in sight until they veered northeasterly toward Fort Sill, located in the middle of Indian Territory as the maps identified it. The river not only kept them on course but assured a reliable water supply for men and horses.

The unseasonably warm weather was holding, but the chill that settled in after each sunset painted their bedrolls with white frost and forced them to keep the campfire burning throughout the night. The burr oak and cottonwood and smaller trees that lined parts of the twisting river afforded welcome windbreaks, and dead branches, especially the long-burning and hot-coaled oaks, made their nights tolerable.

It was midmorning of their fifth day since departing Cal's ranch, and they had the horses moving at a lazy canter across the barren plains that lay next to the river bottom. He figured they should be within two days of the military outpost now. They were a week into February, and Josh found himself getting restless to complete his work at Fort Sill and ride on to locate Quanah and, more particularly, Michael and Tabby. He found himself increasingly anxious about Jael Chernik's predictable resistance to his plan to take Michael home, wherever that was. It occurred to him the only homes he had known since Cassie's death were hotel rooms and dozens of campsites scattered about the Staked Plains and eastern New Mexico. He would need to acquire a residence in Santa Fe.

First, of course, Michael must be made to understand that Josh was his father and that he had no choice about where he was going to live. Josh knew that his claim to fatherhood, as far as Michael was concerned, was a distant second to that of a slain Comanche warrior, Four Eagles. He had been the husband of She Who Speaks, the widowed woman he knew as mother. It saddened him that Cassie would likely never have a serious place in the boy's heart. Michael would only know the mother who gave him life through Josh's own words and, perhaps, those of a few others who had known and loved the gentle, vibrant woman.

First, he must reclaim his son. Jael worried him a lot. She was smart and wily, and seemingly fearless when forced into a corner. She was not a woman likely to resign herself to defeat. She was devising a plan. He knew it. He had to get to Quanah's village soon to nip it in the bud. Strangely, he was anxious to see the woman again, although he looked upon her as his adversary. He promised himself he would be generous in allowing her to visit Michael. Once she could be trusted, he might consent to Michael staying with her on occasion wherever she might live. Hopefully, that would be near Fort Sill, as an employee of the firm.

Oliver Wolf's voice yanked him back to the present. "Have you been hearing that?"

"Hearing what?" Josh asked.

"Gunfire," Cal said. "Maybe half mile up the river."

"Exchange of fire," Wolf said, his voice emotionless. "Folks are shooting at each other up that way. I'll take a look. You might want to ride at a walk until I get back."

"Suit yourself," Cal said. "I'm not in a big rush to meddle into somebody else's fight. I'd at least like to know who the good guys are."

"It's not so easy to tell sometimes," the Cherokee said before he nudged his big stallion into a gallop and rode off.

Cal and Josh slowed the pace of their mounts and the two pack horses. "Strange fellow that one. Sure as hell don't talk much," Cal said.

"He's a man to listen to when he does speak. He was a Confederate major during the war . . . brevet rank, I gather. He's an artist, too, you know."

"You mean like one of those guys who paints pictures? I'll be damned."

Josh could not understand why Cal always played the clown or the ignoramus. He was probably the smartest of the Rivers clan. "I gather he does a little of everything. He sculpts and does pencil drawings and paints, as well. Jessica's going to let him sell some of his work at the theatre."

"Jessica? I wouldn't want a man like that hanging around my woman. That Cherokee's muscled like the stallion he rides . . . probably got a stud tool that'd shame that little guy of yours. Jess is going to lose interest in you real fast."

"Jess and I are just friends. And these days our friendship is entirely platonic."

"See? What did I tell you?"

"I can see why Erin needs a break from you."

"Got to admit she don't always appreciate my sense of humor. She'll miss me though, and we'll make up for our separation when we connect back up. She can't stay away from me long, and I'll be damned if she's not the best blanket partner in New Mexico. You know I ain't had no other woman since I married her."

"Did it ever occur to you that's the way it's supposed to be?"

"Well, the Indians don't see it that way. Mormons don't, either, so I hear tell. I understand about being faithful and all that. But who's to say a man can't be faithful to three or four wives and still be righteous?"

"What about a woman doing the same thing?"

Cal roared in mock horror. "Nope, can't do that. Says so in the Bible, I'm pretty damned sure."

"I doubt you've ever read a chapter of the Bible. I don't know if you ever sat still long enough to learn to read when Mom was teaching us. How'd we get on this subject anyway? You always drag me into the stupidest conversations."

Before Cal could respond, Josh caught sight of a whirlwind of dust headed their way. "It looks like Oliver's in a hurry."

Josh studied the rider and his stallion as they approached. He was forced to agree with Cal. Man and beast were a matched pair. They moved in a single, fluid motion across the prairie, making Josh think of the mythic Centaur, half-man, half-horse.

Wolf's face betrayed nothing, as he pulled Owl up in front of the Rivers brothers. He spoke matter-of-factly. "A mix of young Comanche and Kiowa . . . likely strays from the reservation . . . are hidden in some low bluffs and rocks and have some soldiers trapped in the trees on this side of the river. It looks like a stalemate right now. The soldiers have cover from the trees, and the attackers have the advantage of elevation and the rocks. It doesn't appear either side is drawing blood."

"How many soldiers?" Josh asked.

"No more than ten."

"And the renegades?"

"About the same, maybe a few more. There's something else you might find interesting. I'm certain Colonel Mackenzie's with the soldiers. He's pacing in and out of the trees like a nervous hound. Acts like he's bullet proof. He's not a patient man. Sooner or later, he'll be leading his soldiers up the slope to face his enemy head-on."

"Any ideas on how we help him out?"

"The Comanche and Kiowa are not much more than boys. I don't think it will take a lot to push them on their ways back to the reservation."

21

THEY HAD RIDDEN cautiously along the bank of the Red River, staying in the trees and undergrowth where they could. When they came to a promising river crossing, Cal dropped off and rode across the river. He would cross again when he had passed the site of the skirmish, and then he would try to strike the young renegades from the other side. A little further along, Wolf dismounted his stallion in the trees and then grabbed his Winchester from its scabbard and raced away toward the bluffs.

The plan was to confuse the renegades with gunfire from all sides and to deliver the illusion of superior force. Wolf thought they could chase off the young, would-be warriors without killing anyone, but, of course, they were prepared to take lives if circumstances required. As the combatants came within his sight, Josh hitched his buckskin gelding to a cottonwood sapling and surveyed the scene. He noted a cluster of limestone rocks within rifle range of the Indians that would allow him to launch an attack from the side. Cal should be positioned on the other side soon, and Wolf would be moving in from behind. Wolf might need to climb some, but he would end up on higher ground and could rain bullets downslope on the renegades. Since Wolf had the most tedious journey, they had agreed to wait for his gunfire first.

Josh had no difficulty reaching his firing station unseen. The renegades were obviously focused on the besieged soldiers. Studying his adversaries, he was surprised to find Wolf's statement about the youth of the warriors was an understatement. Half were no more than boys of thirteen or fourteen years, he guessed, and he doubted any were more than seventeen. Ironic that General Mackenzie, the renowned Indian fighter and Comanche nemesis, was pinned down by a war party of mere boys.

The crack of a rifle sounded from higher in the bluffs and then another from Cal's proximity. Josh joined the chorus, carefully aiming to avoid hitting any of the potential targets. In a matter of minutes the young war party was in total disarray, the boys scrambling about in confusion, unable to locate the new enemy. An older boy broke from the group and raced in panic for the horses, which were hidden behind the bluffs. The others took his cue and followed. Wolf had located the horses on his scouting foray, however, and by now would have run them off. The hapless renegades would have a long walk back to the reservation and would think twice about taking up the war path again.

As soon as the Indian scourge was disposed of, the rescuers retrieved their mounts and led them toward the congregated soldiers, who had emerged from the woods now. A lean, starved-looking man with a colonel's insignia on his shoulders walked toward them. From the officer's disfigured hand and missing fingers, Josh knew this was the notorious Brevet General Ranald Slidell Mackenzie. He looked like anything but a colonel or "The general," as his troops usually called him. His mustache was badly in need of a trim, and his cheeks had been untouched by a razor for a week. His general appearance, to describe it kindly, would be unkempt, Josh thought. And his troops appeared to follow their commander's example. Evidently, "spit and polish" was not the General's credo.

As the general drew nearer, Josh found himself struck by the man's eyes, piercing, cobalt-blue with a wild look that made a man wonder if a bit of insanity did not lurk there. They were also eyes that were constantly evaluating and appraising and would not miss much. Don't try to deceive this man, Josh decided instantly.

Mackenzie headed straight for Wolf with his good hand extended. "White Wolf," he said in a scratchy voice that sounded old for a man in his mid-thirties. "What are you doing here? I heard you'd left the scouting service."

"I did. I've taken a temporary job with Josh Rivers here." Wolf introduced Cal and Josh to Mackenzie.

"Well, you came along at a good time. The way those Indians took off, I thought a full company was after them."

"That's what we hoped they'd think," Josh said. He didn't bother to explain the so-called warriors were a bunch of kids. "I must say, General, we were surprised to find you here, especially with such a small contingent."

"I just finished an unofficial visit to Fort Sill. We didn't want to attract attention. We're headed back to Fort Concho, where I am to prepare for my reassignment to Sill."

"You're going to be stationed at Fort Sill?"

"Yes, why don't you gentlemen join me at the fire. I've got a mess sergeant with me who will be making some coffee and breaking out some hardtack if you're hungry enough to eat the stuff. I'm sure as hell not."

The soldiers had several fires going by this time, and the warmth was pleasant as they sat down with Mackenzie at his fire. Steaming cups of coffee were soon placed in their hands, and Josh was anxious to follow up on Mackenzie's mention of his assignment to Fort Sill. "General, you were saying you are assuming duties at Fort Sill. May I ask the nature of those duties, sir? Or is this a military secret?"

Mackenzie gave a wry smile, revealing stained, yellow teeth. "I'm not certain the military has secrets. The master sergeant usually knows what's happening before the highest general, I've found. But, no, it's no secret. General Phillip Sheridan, Commander of the Military Division of the Missouri, in his infinite wisdom, has seen fit to appoint me commanding officer of Fort Sill. As a part of those duties I will be in command of the Comanche-Kiowa and Cheyenne-Arapaho reservations. I am to assume command mid-March."

"My congratulations, General."

"Sympathies would be more in order. Now that the Comanche wars are ending, I had hoped to be assigned to a command in Arizona to fight Apache. This is a dead end in my career. I will never command a fighting unit again. Don't misunderstand me. I will do my duty, and

I will try to bring some order to the reservation mess. First, of course, we need to bring the Kwahadi in."

"General, we may be able to help each other on that score. I have had communications with the Kwahadi."

Mackenzie's eyes came alive and bored in on Josh's. "Tell me about this."

Josh gave him a brief history of his relationship with Quanah, explaining, also, that his son had been taken captive as an infant and was now a part of the Kwahadi band.

"I'll be damned," Mackenzie said, shaking his head in disbelief. "A Comanche chief with his own lawyer. You say he has terms before he comes in. You do know he's not in a position to dictate terms? The starve and destroy strategy of General William Tecumseh Sherman and General Sheridan, much as I detested implementing it, has worked."

"I won't challenge your generals as to strategy. They wreaked the same kind of havoc on the South during the war. Sherman's march through Georgia may live in infamy. The immediate objective was accomplished, I guess, but I suspect the wounds will fester for a century or more. I'll leave that for history to work out. I'm not a soldier, and I won't debate the strategies of war, but I think Quanah can be an instrument of long-term peace."

Mackenzie said, "I just recently learned that Quanah is a half-breed. His mother was a captive white girl by the name of Cynthia Ann Parker. She and Quanah's sister were taken by rangers in a raid on a Comanche village and returned to relatives. Cynthia could no longer speak much resembling English, but she made it clear she wanted to return to the Kwahadi. Mother and daughter died virtual prisoners among a family they did not recognize. I am going to write to family to learn more about them. Perhaps, Quanah would be interested when the time is right." He shifted the conversation quickly. "Now, what does Quanah want?"

"It is mostly a matter of what he does not want. He does not want the chiefs to be imprisoned in the ice house as they have been. He does not want the horses taken and killed. They will surrender their rifles, but he wants to be allowed to keep their bows and traditional weapons, so they can hunt. He wants land set aside specifically for the Kwahadi band, along with cattle to graze the land. He hasn't said so in so many words, but he aspires ultimately to be the leader of the Comanche in peace. He can be your ally in maintaining calm on the reservation. Take my word for it. This man has remarkable political skills."

"As a soldier, I have admired Quanah and the Kwahadi, and, believe it or not, I have a certain fondness for them because of their perseverance and skills at war. I respect the Kwahadi above all the Indians I have fought."

"There is something else. You may call it what you want, but the Comanche will not consider this a surrender. They will just choose to come to the reservation. There will be no treaty with Quanah's band. No formal surrender."

"I suppose we can allow Quanah to label the Kwahadi trek to the reservation whatever he wishes. Our politicians and the press will call this a surrender."

"I understand that."

"These things Quanah wants . . . some I can control, and others I cannot. When I return to Fort Sill, I must also deal with J.M. Haworth the Quaker Indian agent. He is the highest civilian authority at the agency, and the one most likely to launch complaints to the bureaucrats and politicians if he disapproves of what is taking place. As near as I know, he's a good man, though, and I am optimistic we can procure his cooperation. I don't like this business of slaughtering the horses . . . the hardest order for an old horse soldier to carry out. I will have some autonomy in such matters when I assume command at Fort Sill. Still, for appearances sake, we may have to take the horses when the Kwahadi and their allies arrive, and then discreetly return them later. You will need to explain such things to Quanah. We will have to take some care not to convey the appearance of favoring Quanah over the other bands and tribes."

"But, in fact, you will."

The colonel shrugged. "A new commander has some leeway in establishing new policies that will apply to all. It just happens that Quanah's Kwahadi are the first being affected by the changes."

"You sound a bit like a politician yourself, General."

Mackenzie gave a restrained smile and winked. "In this man's army, a good politician will rise in the ranks much faster than the great military tactician, I assure you. Alas, my impolitic ways have made it very difficult to recover my lost star."

"I don't want to wear out my welcome, General, but can I convey to Quanah that you will be receptive to his demands?"

"The chiefs will not be imprisoned, so long as they cooperate. I will spare the horses. I will seriously consider the other matters and do what I can within reason. He will need to have some patience. Just get that son of a bitch to come in. Talk to Dr. Sturm. I am going to send him out in April with a delegation to convince Quanah to come in, although it doesn't sound like it will take much convincing. You work out the details."

Josh had met Dr. Jacob J. Sturm, a physician with dubious credentials, who was married to a Caddo woman, and sometimes served as an interpreter and negotiator for both military and civilian authorities. "We're on our way to Fort Sill now, although much of my mission has been accomplished today. I'll meet with Dr. Sturm and take care of some business matters. Then, if the good weather holds, we'll head out to find Quanah."

Mackenzie dumped his coffee, which had been barely touched, on the ground and got up, signaling their conversation was ended. "It has been a pleasure meeting you, Mr. Rivers. I'm sure our paths will cross again soon. Send my regards to your client."

22

TABITHA RIVERS COULD not shake the feeling that Jael was up to something. They still physically shared a tipi in the Kwahadi village, but since her return from Santa Fe, Jael had become increasingly distant, almost secretive. After Tabitha's arrival as a captive, the young women had formed a fast friendship, a bond that was tightened by the bizarre fact that Jael's adopted son was Tabitha's blood nephew. Tabitha had, with a few exceptions, avoided talking about the inevitable conflict between Jael and Josh over the former Flying Crow's fate.

Things had changed now that the conflict was imminent, and she supposed that was the source of much of the tension between them. Barring a few belligerent holdouts, the People accepted that spring would find them trudging on the trail to the reservation. Their days of freedom to roam the vast Llano Estacado were ending.

A way of life was near death. From the gloom and quiet that had already descended on the village, it was obvious the mourning had already begun.

Tabitha knelt before the tipi fire, roasting horse ribs on the coals that were covered by a shield of tiny flickering flames. It was nearly sundown, but the fire helped preserve the sun's warmth and it was comfortable in the skin-sheathed abode. The aroma of the sweet meat stirred her hunger, and she smiled at how she had vomited up her first meal of horse flesh a few months earlier. She was glad she had sent Smokey to Santa Fe with Jael. While she had adapted to the notion that a horse could also be a meat animal, the thought of eating an equine friend or acquaintance still bordered on cannibalism as far as she was concerned.

She felt the draft of an open tipi flap before she turned and saw Michael slip through the opening. Like his Comanche brethren he moved quietly by habit. She looked up at him and saw Josh as a boy. The rust-colored hair, the green-brown eyes, the perfectly carved lips. There could be no denying his parentage. And, of course, Jael was past denying that.

"Hello, Michael. Are you hungry? Supper will be ready soon." He was always "Michael" now, ever since Jael completed her mission in Santa Fe, and English and occasional Spanish were the only languages permitted to be spoken in the tipi these days. The boy's English was near perfect for one not yet seven years, although some of his conversational English was a bit formal.

"I am hungry, yes, Aunt Tabby." He placed his small bow and quiver near his sleeping robe at the edge of the tipi and then joined her near the fire. He was a remarkable boy, she thought, evidently carrying his mother's aptitude for languages. And then she remembered that the skill could not be a matter of biology. She forgot sometimes that Michael had a first mother, as she now thought of Cassie, who had been murdered and raped by members of this very band, perhaps, even by Four Eagles, the boy's adoptive father. She had been there that day and been a captive herself before escaping into the rapids of the Canadian River.

"Where is your mother?"

"She said she must speak with Quanah. She will be—" He paused, struggling for a word. "Late. We must eat. She will eat when she comes late."

She smiled at the boy. He no longer looked like a Comanche. Jael had insisted his hair be cut in the style of white boys, and Tabitha had helped with the task, not an easy one when the only cutting implement was a skinning knife. The result was a bit ragged, and he had not been especially compliant. Afterward, some of his Comanche friends taunted him, said he had been scalped by women. He bore up well, however, and he had a way of putting things behind him that was enviable.

Tabitha wondered why Jael, who seemed to think of herself as Comanche despite her Jewishness, was in such a rush to convert Michael to a white boy. She had even somehow acquired some boy's clothing on her trip, as well as a few items for herself. It was like she was preparing for a Comanche masquerade ball. Yes, Jael had something in mind, and she wasn't talking these days.

"You did not find any rabbits?" Tabitha asked the boy, stating the obvious.

"No. The rabbits have gone away with the deer and the buffalo. We have only horses to eat. And they are not many. Mother had ten horses. Four we have eaten. What happens after we eat all the horses?"

Most Comanche women marry, often to become second or third wives, upon losing a husband. The deceased warrior's horses were given to the new husband as sort of a dowry. Since Jael, the former She Who Speaks, did not take a husband, she was permitted to claim his horses as her own, a choice she may not have had if not for her special relationship with Quanah.

"It is almost March. Buffalo will return with the grass. So will deer. We will have meat in our lodges again." She was not as optimistic as she sounded, but she figured things could not be much worse, and the change of seasons would allow hunters to range further in search of wild game. There were too many Comanche and assorted other bands encamped here to feed from the hunt alone. She hoped the final peace terms would be agreed upon soon, so the trek to Fort Sill could begin. She feared many from the remnants of other bands and Kiowa would starve. While the Kwahadi were generous in their sharing, they also took care of the true People first.

"I do not understand March and April and months. Spring, I understand. Seasons are not so hard," Michael said.

"It is confusing, but you do very well."

The sizzling horse ribs lay over a forked stick and Tabitha pulled it from the fire and offered the meat to Michael. After waiting for it to cool, he took his small skinning knife from its sheath and separated several of the ribs and pressed them to his lips, seemingly savoring the fragrance before tearing the meat off the bone with his teeth. Tabitha cut off some pieces for herself and they sat there silently, chewing the dry, leathery meat and gnawing the bones naked until they devoured it all. They were both still hungry after what was cooked was gone, but what remained was set aside for Jael to eat when she returned.

Michael finally broke the silence. "I will go to my robe, Aunt Tabby. Mother said I must sleep early."

"Goodnight, Michael." This was strange. It was several hours before his usual bedtime. But the boy was not a rebellious child. Most Comanche children were not. The People raised obedient children, a necessity, she supposed, if they were going to survive the perils of the prairie, especially during these last days of freedom.

23

ICHAEL HAD BEEN asleep for several hours when Jael returned to the tipi. Tabitha immediately started roasting the remaining horse meat. By the time her friend joined her at the fire, it was ready to eat, given that Jael, like most others of her adoptive band, preferred the surface charred and the flesh underneath more raw than rare.

"Quanah kept you late," Tabitha remarked, struggling to start a conversation.

"We had much to discuss. The exodus from freedom is on the horizon."

"You speak of this so negatively. Your people will be fed. There will be no more war."

"The People will depend upon a government from Washington for their food and shelter and protection. Dependency is not freedom. Quanah knows this, and he grieves. But he has no choice. One must first survive, and he believes he can fight for a different kind of freedom. And to that end he will battle for self-sufficiency for the People."

"And I will write of Quanah and you and the People and try to persuade others to support policies that will allow this to happen."

"I know you will. You are a good person and a friend of the People. You are also my friend."

"I wasn't certain. If I may be blunt, you have been cold and distant since your return from Santa Fe."

"I know. I have been very troubled. But that is not an excuse for my behavior. You are like a sister to me. Believe that, no matter what happens. I will never forget you."

"You make it sound like something terrible is going to happen. It has to do with Michael, doesn't it?"

"I would never let anything happen to Michael."

"Not intentionally. But you are not going to surrender him to Josh, either."

"No, I will not."

"But there has to be a way. Josh is Michael's father. His wife and mother were brutally murdered and raped by your people. Michael was abducted. He was stolen from a loving family. That was not Josh's fault. Can you blame him for wanting his son back?"

Jael stared into the fading embers of the fire for several moments before tossing a few more sticks on the coals. "No," she said, in a voice that seemed emotionless, "I cannot blame him. Josh is a good man, better than good. I am sorry that life brought him such tragedy. But the Great Spirit, or whatever force governs this world, placed Michael in my care, and I am his mother in the real sense, even more than Josh is his father. I truly believe this."

"The law will not agree."

"I know this. And I cannot live without Michael. It would be less painful for me to end my life. And I considered this."

"You don't mean that. Suicide?"

"It is the coward's path. And it would do yet more harm to Michael. I thought of this only briefly. I say it only so you can understand how desperate I am. I hope you will think less harshly of me when I make choices you do not like."

"What do you mean? Josh is my brother. Michael is my nephew. As much as I care about you, I could not betray Josh."

"I appreciate that. And I have tried not to put you in that position these past months. Now, I am very tired. I must sleep."

Tabitha lay awake for several hours that night, troubled by things Jael had said, feeling frustrated and powerless to help either her brother or her friend. Finally, her eyes closed and she fell into a deep slumber. When she awoke at sunrise, she found that the fire had died, leaving the tipi ice-cold in its wake. She cast her eyes about the tipi, wondering why Jael, as was her routine, had not tossed some wood on the fire in the middle of the night. It was only then she realized Jael and Michael were gone.

24

AFTER HER MEETING with Quanah, Jael, with the help of Growling Bear and Scratching Turkey, had saddled her dun mare and Michael's pinto gelding with Comanche frame saddles and loaded the two pack animals with most of the belongings she had sneaked out of the tipi the past several days. She had prevailed upon Quanah to give Tabitha the remaining few horses in her diminished herd for food, currency or riding, as she chose. Quanah had promised to assure Tabitha's safety.

After Tabitha had fallen asleep, Jael stealthily took the Henry rifle and ammunition and rolled up her buffalo robe. Then she had gently awakened Michael and gathered up his robe and the few items she had not already loaded, and they quickly ducked through the tipi flap and raced for the two warriors and awaiting horses. She was grateful Tabitha had not awakened. She did not want an unpleasant scene. She regretted having to confiscate her friend's rifle and knew she would be angry. Weapons were more than a means of hunting or defending oneself for Tabitha. She had an affection for them that went beyond their usefulness, and the Henry was her prize. She would regret now she had taught Jael how to fire the rifle.

Michael had been puzzled by their departure from the village and at first complained, reverting to Comanche in his protestations until he realized his mother would not respond to words spoken in his native tongue. She had not forewarned the boy of her plans, fearful he would inadvertently tell Tabitha. For now, she told him, they had to leave or they would be separated from each other at the reservation. She promised to explain in the days ahead.

Quanah had insisted that Growing Bear and Scratching Turkey accompany her for two days. Thereafter, she would be on her own. She felt guilty deserting Quanah and her Kwahadi band. She knew her interpreting skills would be valuable when they started the trail to reservation life. She was particularly saddened by giving up the chance to be a part of the Rivers and Sinclair office near the reservation. But her son came first.

Then there was Josh Rivers. She nearly cried at the thought of what he would think when he learned what she had done. She could not deny that she cared where she stood in his esteem, and she knew the pain she was inflicting by escaping was unforgivable. She was drawn to him in some way she could not fathom. That night he kissed her was seared in her memory, and she could not escape it. But she must overcome this weakness she had for him, for she had no doubt he would use it take her son from her.

For two days, they rode across dry prairie that seemed to raise only dirt, she thought. She supposed grass would work its way through the earth as spring came on, but Growling Bear explained that buffalo did not stay long in this country because their visits quickly gnawed the grass to roots. There were some scrub trees and brush along the creeks and river banks and more healthy growth in some of the larger canyons that crisscrossed like giant spider webs across the barren land. Her warrior guards explained as they rode that she should never stray far from a canyon that offered a flowing creek, where she could find water and, usually, shelter. She noticed most of the creek beds yielded up only white, powdery dust, and she was told that rains were rare in this part of what the whites called Texas. She was instructed that due south the creeks would empty into a larger river that would lead to a white eyes' fort. From what Jael had learned from maps she had seen in Santa Fe, this should be a branch of the Concho River, and the military outpost would be Fort Concho, with a budding town of San Angelo sprouting up nearby.

After the third sunrise, the two warriors prepared to leave. By now Jael had relented and permitted Flying Crow, as they still called him, to converse in Comanche with their friends, and he was trying to convince Growling Bear to stay with them. "He must obey his chief," Jael explained to the boy. "You know this."

"You have been good friends and protectors," she told the warriors in Comanche. "I thank you. And I will never forget you."

Growling Bear tapped his fist gently on his chest, signaling his friendship. "She Who Speaks is a great warrior woman. Four Eagles was my friend, and I would have gladly taken you in as my third wife. But I knew you would break your own trail. It is our destiny to meet again. I know not where or when, but until then, may the Great Spirit ride with you."

As the warriors mounted their horses and galloped away, Jael could not remember when she had felt more alone. She turned to Michael, who stared up at her with wide, somber eyes, looking like a puppy that had been swatted for misbehaving. It reminded her there were no dogs remaining in the village. They had all been eaten. "All will be well, Michael," she said, reassuringly.

"I am afraid, Mother, and I do not understand why we do this."

An hour or so before nightfall, they came upon a canyon carved out of the middle of the prairie. She could see a stream snaking its way through the canyon floor, and the walls seemed to extend for several miles. It was no more than a half mile wide and shallow in comparison to Palo Duro. She quickly found a wide trail that led to the floor, troubled only a little by numerous hoofprints of horses in the dust, some shoed and some not, indicating the canyon had frequent visitors.

By sunset, she had found a cave large enough for the two of them, less than four feet high and no deeper, but large enough to break the nipping wind that was now whipping down the canyon walls. There was game in the canyon as well. They had each contributed a rabbit with their archery skills. Not knowing if there might be other canyon occupants downstream, she did not wish to use the rifle, although Tabitha had taught her to fire it efficiently. She was not nearly as proficient as her instructor, though. The thought of Tabby reminded her of how angry her friend would be at the loss of her Henry rifle. She guessed taking the rifle made her a thief, and the thought was not pleasing.

As they ate the roasted rabbit meat, Michael broke the silence that had prevailed since Growling Bear and Scratching Turkey turned back. Any words between them had been terse and perfunctory. "Mother, I do not like it away from the People. Where do we go?"

She scooted closer to him. "It is time for you to understand. You should also have some choice in this matter. If you truly wish to go back after I explain, we shall do so. You understand that you are Josh Rivers's son, do you not?"

"You have told me this. But how can that be? Four Eagles was my father. Can a person have two fathers?"

"Yes. A father is a man who loves and cares for you and raises you as his own. But a father can also be one who gave life to you by mating with a woman."

"Like a stallion and a mare? I know how babies come to be."

"Look at yourself. Your hair is from Josh, and your eyes and so many things. You were taken from him by a war party when you were not much more than a baby. If you had not been taken, you would have had only one father and one mother."

"Because you did not mate with Josh Rivers? Then do I have two mothers?"

"You had another mother once. Like Four Eagles, she died. But you do not remember her because you were so small. Now you have one father and one mother. Do you understand this?"

"Yes. You are the mother who raised me, like Four Eagles was my father."

"You are Comanche. A part of you always will be, but the soldiers will see you as a white boy, and if we go to the reservation, you will be taken from the Comanche. I will be taken also because, like you, I had two mothers and two fathers, and my blood is not considered Comanche by the white people."

"Then we can be together."

"No. That will not be. You will be returned to your father."

"But you can come with us."

"That cannot be. You and he have family. I am not of that family. He is a good man, a kind man, and I believe he would let me visit you sometimes. But you would no longer live with me, and I fear someday you would forget me. Someday, though, you would be happy with the Rivers family, just as I became happy with the Comanche. These people would care for you and love you. I am taking you away because I am selfish. I want you for myself. I cannot promise this is best for you."

"We do not go back. I do not know this father, but I know this mother. I go with you. But where is that?"

"We go to a place called San Angelo. It is near a soldiers' fort. The whites call it Fort Concho. I do not think they would expect us to be near soldiers. I hope they would not look for us there."

"Someone would try to find us?"

"Yes, your father, Josh Rivers. He is not a man who quits. He will look for you."

"Why did you not ask Quanah to kill him when he came to our village?"

"He was Quanah's friend, and he was helping our people. "

"If he finds us, you should kill him. I will help you."

"No. He is your father."

"I gave him a crow feather. Now I am sorry. I will not go with him. I hate him."

Her response was firm. "You must come to understand him whatever happens. He seeks you because he loves you. You are not allowed to hate him. Never."

25

SHORTLY BEFORE THE sun crawled over the canyon rim, Jael was awakened by the sound of loud voices echoing from downstream. Michael was sleeping soundly rolled in his robe, which had been spread out next to the cave wall beside hers. She decided to carefully follow the stream and determine who the visitors were. She hated to disturb Michael, but she did not want him to awaken and then call for her because she was missing. That would alert whomever was sharing the canyon with them.

"Michael," she said softly, shaking his shoulder gently and pressing a finger to her lips when his head popped from the robe. He looked at her with sleepy eyes, and in Comanche told her it was cold and too early to get up.

She replied, using English. "Go back to sleep if you wish, but stay here. I must go search for something. Be very, very quiet."

Again, speaking Comanche, he promised he would and burrowed back into his robe. This was not the time for her to scold him for his choice of languages, she decided.

She got up and tucked the Army Colt under the crude belt that held up her doeskin britches, the cold iron feeling like ice pressed against her thigh. Then she snatched up the Henry, half-slid down the rocky slope to the bank of the stream and began inching her way through the prickly cedars that had taken up root in this part of the canyon. Fortunately, the cover afforded by the cedars had not been diminished by the onset of winter. The voices grew louder, and she could tell they were sharply laced with anger. She caught sight of a canvas-covered wagon through a break in the trees and instantly dropped to the ground. The early morning sun cast full light on the campsite now, and as she crawled closer, she could make out four men, two dark, thickly bearded men leaning against the wagon, evidently watching a dispute between the other two.

The two who were at odds spoke Spanish, and they were clearly arguing over a woman. One man said she would bring a great price as a virgin, and the other said he did not give a damn. He had waited too long. And he was the boss. The man arguing for protecting the merchandise was younger and smooth-shaven. She guessed his lineage would be a mix of Spanish and Indian, as she had heard many Mexicans were. The other man was older and bulkier, clearly white with his ash-blond hair and thick mustache and ruddy complexion showing through the week-old growth of whiskers. They were obviously Comancheros. She had seen such men many times when they visited the village with goods to trade, sometimes offering small children for sale.

Suddenly, the older man slipped his pistol from its holster and pointed it at the younger man, who raised his hands, signaling he was not going to fight about the matter any longer. The blond man squeezed the trigger and the gun exploded, its bullet drilling a bloody hole in his antagonist's forehead before he crumpled to the earth. He turned to his companions, swinging his weapon challengingly. They shrugged and walked away from the wagon toward a small remuda of horses some twenty paces away. One of the men began to saddle his horse, but the other stopped and turned around, appearing to be interested in what the big blond man was going to do.

Then she saw what the argument was all about. The man reached down and yanked a naked girl from the ground, clutching her long hair and dragging her stumbling toward the wagon, leaving no doubt about his intent. Jael thought the girl could be no more than thirteen. She was tall for her age, possibly close to Jael's own five and a half feet, but she was thin, just short of emaciated, her breasts no more than pre-pubescent nubs. This animal was not going to rape the girl. The fair thing was to give the man warning, she supposed, as she chambered a cartridge into the Henry and aimed. She squeezed the trigger and fired a bullet into his meaty buttocks. He shrieked and released the girl and turned just as she drove another missile into his chest. So much for fair.

The man who had been watching the scene unfold pulled his six-gun and ran toward his companion, hunched over, his head bobbing and his eyes searching for the source of the gunfire. Jael delivered two more quick shots, and he fell forward, face down in the dirt. The other Comanchero finished mounting his horse and disappeared into the timber. He was moving like a man not looking for trouble.

Jael slipped out of the trees and into the campsite, slowly approaching the girl, who was struggling to get up, as she stared wide-eyed at Jael. The girl was filthy, and the side of her face was badly bruised, but even this could not hide the promise of blossoming into beauty one day. Jael was shocked when she saw the crisscrosses of raw and bloody welts and scratches across her narrow back. The girl's eyes and hair were dark like her own, but Jael was not certain she was Mexican. "Do you speak English?" she asked.

The girl stood up, her body erect and proud, seemingly not embarrassed by her nakedness. "Yes, ma'am, I speak English and passable Spanish." She hesitated. "You're a lady."

Jael could not resist a smile. "Some might dispute that. I suppose my behavior wasn't very ladylike just now. Are there some clothes for you in the wagon? We need to get something on you before you freeze to death."

"Yes, ma'am." She moved toward the wagon and climbed into the back, where she started to sift through an assortment of garments that were apparently being hauled for trade or sale by the renegades. The wagon bed was nearly packed full, Jael observed. Cooking utensils, a small selection of Dutch ovens, half a dozen rifles and a supply of ammunition, food supplies, and many cases of liquor.

Shortly, the girl emerged from the wagon with a pair of long johns, an orange blouse, and a flowery cotton skirt. She had also found some hard-soled moccasin-like footwear that seemed to suit her. She quickly slipped into the underwear which did not fit her all that badly. The skirt seemed fine, but the blouse hung on her boney frame.

"I suppose the long johns aren't fashionable," the girl said, "but they're practical for keeping warm or riding a horse, if you know what I mean."

This was one tough young lady, Jael thought. On the other hand, the soft ones probably didn't survive out on these plains. Jael extended her hand, "I'm Jael Chernik."

The girl took her hand in a surprisingly firm grip. "I'm Rylee O'Brian. And I owe you more than I can ever pay back." Rylee gave a tentative smile, and all at once tears began to roll slowly down her cheeks, washing furrows in her dirt-caked face. Jael stepped forward and took Rylee in her arms, holding her until she was all sobbed out.

Rylee recovered her composure soon. "How did you happen to come along?" Rylee asked.

"My son and I are traveling to San Angelo. We rode into the canyon to set up camp for the night."

"A woman and her boy alone out here in the middle of hell. That seems awfully strange."

"It's a long story. I will explain when we have more time. I need to get back to Michael. But how did you end up with this garbage? You have your own story, and I fear it's not pretty."

"Pa was a school teacher in San Antonio. Mom was Spanish. I never did understand it, but I guess that's different than Mexican somehow, and her family didn't like Pa much because he tainted the blood. So, Pa convinced Mom to leave San Antonio and move northwest to take up ranching now that the Comanche wars were ending. Pa didn't really know a steer from a bull, and we nearly starved out for two years. We were going to pack up and go back to San Antonio this spring when these men came along. They raped and killed Mom, and shot Pa dead when he tried to stop them. They didn't hurt me except to beat me and whip me when I tried to get away. They said I was merchandise. They knew a man who would pay a nice price for girls my age, and if he didn't buy me, they were going to sell me to a whorehouse along the Mexican border."

"I'm sorry. You can come with us until you decide what you want to do. We have much in common."

"It's been a good month now. They left Pa and Mom on the prairie. They didn't even get a decent burial. Took the five horses we had and sold them along the trail. Mom had some family jewelry that's probably stashed in the wagon someplace. Those were about the only things of value we had. Our little cow herd was already disappearing or turning wild. They raped and killed another woman who was home alone a few weeks back. Burned down the place. They said folks would think Comanches had done it."

"We'll give these men the same burial they gave your parents."

Jael studied the wagon and then looked over the horses. "How did you get to this place?"

"We came in from the south. The canyon fades out further down the creek. This was supposed to be a stopover for a few days before we turned back south. I tried to escape last night. Thought it might be my last chance. No idea where I'm at or where I was going, but at least there was water nearby. They caught up with me this morning and dragged me back here and Rudy . . . that was the boss's name . . . stripped me down and took the bullwhip to me again. I guess that's when he decided he wanted me, and he and Rafael started arguing. I think Rafael wanted me for himself, but he was always kind to me and tried to keep the others from hurting me too much. There was a streak of good in him, and like Pa used to say about some folks, he just took the wrong turn at a fork along the trail."

"You've got a team of horses and three riding mounts. I'm not sure I can harness a team. My father let me hold the reins sometimes when I was a little girl, but I have not had any experience handling a team and wagon."

"Oh, that's no problem. I used to help Pa harness the team and drive the wagon all the time at home. Are you thinking we'd take the wagon?"

"Why not? We could sell the contents . . . except for your mom's jewelry . . . in San Angelo. We'd dump the whiskey here. That's trouble, and it would lighten the load for the team to pull. What do you think?"

"I think we're in business, ma'am."

"Call me Jael for now. I may change my name later. I'll explain when we get on the trail. Right now, I need to fetch my son, and you should come with me in case the other Comanchero returns. After that we've got work to do . . . and a lot of thinking."

26

FORT SILL WAS as isolated and drab as Josh remembered, although there were signs of construction scattered about the grounds. An enormous frame structure, shaped somewhat like a barn rose from the red, grainy soil of the prairie. Wolf pointed at the building, "That is Evans' Trading Store. Not much in the way of merchandise when I was last there, but I suppose it takes time to stock a store that large."

Josh's nostrils were struck by a putrid odor that threatened to make him gag. At the same instant, Buck and the other horses grew nervous and restless. "My God, what's that smell?"

"Dead horses. When they come in to the reservation, the soldiers confiscate the Kiowa and Comanche horses and take them south of the post a mile or so and kill them. The ground is littered with decaying horse corpses. That's why I left the Army. Killing men was one thing, but the slaughter of the horses I could not accept. The smell is much worse with the southerly summer winds."

"Maybe this will stop if Mackenzie means what he says."

Cal interjected, "There's always some damn fool up the ladder that knows better than the officer in the field. Mackenzie seems to have good intentions, but intentions ain't worth shit sometimes."

"What's going on at that building?" Josh waved toward a partially completed stone structure nearly a hundred yards beyond the store.

There was a commotion and a cluster of soldiers gathered outside the building, and the three riders, leading their two pack horses, reined their mounts toward the activity. As they approached they saw that the soldiers were carrying baskets containing raw slabs of meat to the open door of the building where several others were pitching the contents through the opening. Armed guards were also posted, and they could hear angry, unintelligible voices coming from inside.

"Do you know what's going on here?" Josh asked Wolf.

"This is where Comanche chiefs are imprisoned. This building was to be an icehouse, but there was not room for all the chiefs in the basement of the guardhouse, so the army decided to lodge the overflow here."

"Do they ever get out to move around?"

"No. One may be released from time to time when someone up the chain of command decides he will no longer be a troublemaker. They are given a ration of raw meat, much of it rotting, daily. Of course, they are not allowed knives to slice it or fires to cook it."

"The building doesn't have a roof on it yet," Cal observed.

"No," Wolf said. "They never got around to that. Be assured, Josh, your Comanche friends have no real advocates up the military chain. Oddly, the greatest Comanche fighter of them all may soon be their greatest benefactor. And Quanah may be to the Comanche what Kicking Bird was to the Kiowa."

Josh winced as the wide, thick door of the icehouse slammed and the iron bars that held it tight were slid into position. "What do you mean?" he asked, as they watched the soldiers parade away.

"Kicking Bird, like Quanah, saw the future and took advantage of it. He worked with the Army to bring other tribesmen to the reservation. The military designated him principal chief of the Kiowa, and he became the intermediary who worked out differences between the reservation Kiowa and the Army. He also rode with the cavalry on occasion on peace missions and persuaded other chiefs to bring their bands in. I met him on several occasions. He was a small, wiry man, lacking the physical stature of most Kiowa, but he had a keen insight into other men, white and Indian, and knew how to reason and persuade and gather support for his ideas."

"A politician, like somebody else I know," Josh said.

"Exactly. Kicking Bird got the rebellious chiefs released from imprisonment and then kept most of them in line . . . with the exception of a few who led their bands from the reservation to join Quanah. Of course, some of the Kiowa chiefs resented him and considered him a traitor. More likely, they were envious."

"I read in the *New Mexican* a year or so ago that he died. He was important enough to make the white newspapers," Josh said.

"Yes, he was less than forty years old and in excellent health seemingly. But that didn't give him immunity to poison."

"Somebody poisoned him?"

"It is not known who. But the post surgeon said it was strychnine."

"I always heard politics is a blood sport," Cal remarked.

27

JOSH DECIDED IT was time to meet with Dr. Jacob Sturm. Cal suggested he and Oliver Wolf might visit a tavern down the road from Sturm's rustic one-room hospital and office while Josh conferred with the self-ordained physician. Wolf was well known at the post, so he was unlikely to encounter any problems with service at the establishment. Besides, he did not partake of alcohol in any form. Cal would drink enough to keep both men welcome. Josh, himself, was no more than an occasional drinker, and if Cal was present, he was ever ready to finish whatever spirits remained in Josh's glass.

The last time Josh visited Sturm, the hospital had been filled with dying patients. Today, the hospital was vacant except for the doctor with a receding hairline and short-cropped beard. The scruffy-looking occupant was slumped over his desk, puffing on a crumpled, rolled cigarette and staring at something invisible on the desktop, which appeared to lack any smooth writing surface. Sturm looked up as Josh stepped nearer to the desk. "Do I know you?" he asked.

Josh extended his hand, which the other man did not seem to notice. "I'm Josh Rivers. We met last summer about negotiating peace terms with Quanah. I'm a lawyer from Santa Fe. I felt you opened a few doors for me at that time."

"Yeah, I sort of remember that now."

I must have made quite an impression, Josh thought.

The man snuffed out the stub of his cigarette on the desktop, which looked like a moldy cheese from the countless pockmarks that dotted it. He immediately pulled a can of tobacco from the drawer and a thin cigarette paper, and with trembling fingers began to roll another. "You know, tobacco was the greatest medicine God ever gave man. Calms the nerves better than any damned drug on the market."

Josh wondered what the man was like without the calming effect of his tobacco.

"Doctor," he said. "I'm here to talk about Quanah again."

Dr. Sturm did not respond until he had lighted his cigarette and started sucking it like a calf on a teat.

"Yes. Quanah. I understand things are going to happen this spring. I heard Bad Hand Mackenzie's going to assume command of Sill then. A barely weaned lieutenant stopped by last week and told me to keep April open because the new commanding officer would need an interpreter to be an emissary to the Comanche. Keep April open. Piss on them. All I got is open time since the Army quit contracting patients to me. Soldiers are all treated by the post surgeon now. They got another army doc to help him."

"I wondered why there were no patients in your hospital."

"Yeah, I used to get the dying and contagious over here, but now the post hospital has built on another ward for that. I still have a few civilians walk in, and the Quaker agent Haworth sends a few Kiowa and Comanche who don't insist on having their medicine man shake a rattle over them. I get a Cheyenne on occasion. Never Arapaho for some reason. But, hell, who am I to complain, we probably save the same number of patients. Those who are going to get well, do. Those who aren't, do not."

A rather cynical man. Josh really wasn't interested in Sturm's healing prowess. He attempted again to turn the conversation to Comanche peace. "I'm confident General Mackenzie is open to treating the Kwahadi more generously than other bands that have come to the reservation. It's not a matter of favoritism, it is a question of policy change." He was not free to quote Mackenzie, but he was sharing the man's expressed thoughts, and he figured it was the best way to broach the subject.

Sturm said, "So, what do I have to do with any of this? I'm just an interpreter. And my Comanche leaves a lot to be desired. I'm just the best they got for a white man."

Josh explained the gist of what Quanah was requesting. "I'm hoping you will encourage Mackenzie to be receptive to those terms. I'm here to answer any concerns you might have about them. You will do yourself and the country a service if you can help bring this about. I plan to be with Quanah when you meet with him in a few months. I will do everything I can to assure your safety. I will be leaving soon to see Quanah."

"I can see no reason to discourage what you are proposing. I think you should meet the Indian agent before you leave. Haworth does the best he can, and he's a decent man. You can probably tell him what you know about Quanah and suggest it would be in their mutual interest to form an alliance of sorts. I can introduce you if you wish."

Finally, Dr. Sturm was being helpful and seemed to have cleared the fog from his head. Perhaps, he was scheming some way he might profit by also teaming up with Quanah. "I would appreciate an introduction before we leave. We hope to be on our way in a few days, weather permitting."

"Weather won't permit. My shoulder's aching like hell today. Don't know a good doctor, do you?" he said, as he snuffed out another cigarette on his desk.

"One other matter before I leave. My firm is looking to set up an office near the reservation. We are planning to represent members of the reservation tribes and develop expertise in the area of Indian affairs. It is possible one of our employees might reside here, and a residence connected to the office would be useful. Most of the housing I see near Fort Sill consists of dugouts and board shacks. Also, my two companions and I have been on the trail for a spell, we wouldn't mind a roof over our heads for a few days."

Dr. Sturm surrendered his first smile of the day, showing a mouth of jumbled tobacco-stained teeth. "Perhaps I can help on both counts. I happen to have three reasonably comfortable beds right here. A fireplace at each end of the room for even heat. I don't furnish breakfast, but the tavern serves meals. I'd say a dollar apiece per night. I guarantee you won't be bothered by patients."

"Sold," Josh said. "What about the office?"

"It so happens I own a property west of the fort grounds that has the Comanche reservation on two sides of it. The roof's falling in, but the walls are made of large limestone blocks. A rancher put it up with the notion of making it Indian proof, so to speak. It didn't do him any good. A band of Kiowa caught him away from the house, but it saved his wife and two boys. A few years later the government bought out her dubious rights in the land, and I purchased a four-acre tract with the house on it."

"You mentioned dubious title to the ranchland. I know something about titles, Doctor. We're in Indian Territory. There's not much in the way of documented title here. You just claim land and see if you can hold it. I'd guess the house is no better."

"Nobody else is laying claim right now. For two hundred dollars, you're not risking much. Of course, you'd have to put that much more into it and chase out the coons and snakes to make the place fit to live and work in, but I'd guess you could gamble that. I always thought I'd fix it up for my family. But I don't have any money and I need some bad."

"We'll take a look tomorrow."

28

THE TWO-STORY HOUSE was easy enough to locate. To the east, the hazy outline of the buildings at Fort Sill could barely be seen on this clear day, and the limestone structure appeared more like a fortress than a residence. There was a small lean-to frame structure, adaptable to a horse shelter, not far from the house, but otherwise the house stood alone on the stark and naked prairie.

They had hitched the horses on the post in front of the house. Wolf was already strolling around the exterior, appraising the stonework, stepping back from time to time and examining the work with an artist's eye. The front view of the house formed an almost perfect square, and there was certainly nothing intricate about the design. Intermittent gun slots were carved out on all sides of the structure. There seemed to be an ample number of windows for natural light, but even these were narrow, presumably to facilitate defense in case of attack. The roof sagged precariously.

When they entered the house, Josh noted the unusual weight and thickness of the formidable oak door. The house had been stripped of any furniture or contents, and Josh had difficulty envisioning how the house might function as both residence and office. However, Wolf seemed genuinely fascinated by the house, climbing the stairs several times, pacing back and forth silently, evidently taking mental measurements of the rooms. Cal, on the other hand, had done a quick walk-through and decided he preferred the company of the horses.

Finally, Josh's curiosity got the best of him. "What are you thinking, Oliver? Could this work for our offices?"

Wolf smiled, his eyes sparkling with excitement. "Work? This could be a fabulous place. It was built for the ages. The size of the stone . . . what a job it must have been to put those in place. I assume, for now, you want to change as little as possible. There are three bedrooms upstairs with adequate size. The roof is on borrowed time, but I do not see any water damage upstairs. Your priority would be to find carpenters to reframe the roof and sheath it with long, thick cedar shingles. I am certain there are carpenters at the post who would be eager to make some money off-duty. The bedrooms don't need anything done for now. The occupants can decide whether to paint or plaster."

"So, what about the main floor?"

"Perfect. The downstairs is a single room, probably for heating convenience. You are still asking a lot of the big fireplace to heat the entire area in a house this size. Fortunately, the fireplace is located at what should be the office area. I would partition off the room into an office section and a living area. The outer door would open directly into the office. A new door to the right of the entry would be cut in the partition wall and would open into the living portion. The stairway to the bedrooms would still come off the residential side. A big combination heating and cook stove could service the residence. You would need to partition off a private office on the business side of the main floor, and that would leave ample staff and reception space, but I would think it would suffice near-term. The beauty of this place is that it would be so simple to build on to almost any part of the house to add space."

"Could you make the arrangements for me?"

"Be glad to. I'll do some drawings this afternoon and then see if I can find one of the carpenters at the fort. After I help you locate Quanah, if you like, I can stop by here before I return to Santa Fe and check on the progress and help for a short spell."

"I would appreciate that. You'll be on the firm payroll till you get back to Santa Fe. I don't see the castle here that you do, but I'll tell Sturm we will buy the place."

Josh's next stop was the Indian agency. Wolf said he was returning to Sturm's hospital to work on the sketches for the house modifications. Cal indicated he might try to get in on a poker game at the tavern.

J. M. Haworth impressed Josh as a competent man, who believed in his work and made the most of the limited resources that came his way. He was a middle-aged man with prematurely white hair and a clean-shaven wind-burned face, who presided over a compound consisting of several large frame buildings and assorted scattered shacks, all of which were in a state of disrepair. Josh guessed the larger buildings were warehouses. Indians, mostly male, sat in clusters about the grounds. Many had blankets tugged over their shoulders to ward off the chill of a wind that had started to come up a few hours earlier. Some of the Indians were engaged in conversation, but many just sat silently on the crusty ground, staring at something on the horizon unseen by anyone else. This is the home of broken spirits, Josh thought.

Haworth had invited him into the small plank-walled building that served as the agent's office. A wood stove kept the building tolerable, but the bitter wind slipped easily between gaps in the boards. Burlap sacks tacked to portions of the walls did not seem to block all that much of nature's blasts.

Haworth sat in a rickety straight-back chair behind a decrepit desk covered with stacks of paper. Josh's identical chair on the other side was equally unstable, but after struggling a bit, he maneuvered his feet to hold it steady. He had told Haworth about Quanah's requests, deciding not to frame the concerns as demands. The agent had no say-so about policies. He was charged simply with the responsibility of carrying out the orders of generally less informed, and occasionally corrupt, men.

Haworth said, "I have never liked the senseless slaughter of the horses, and, of course, the treatment of the chiefs is abhorrent to men of any sincere religious convictions. I have protested to the Army and to my civilian superiors but to no avail."

"I have reason for optimism that Mackenzie will address some of these issues to your satisfaction."

"I can only pray that he will."

"My main reason for stopping by was to lay groundwork for a fruitful relationship between you and Quanah. You will find him far different than the angry and barbaric villain he has been painted in the press and by many in the military. Mackenzie respects him and, surprisingly, sees him in an optimistic light."

"My faith believes in redemption and welcomes any man to embrace peace. His past is no barrier to a true friendship between us. Kicking Bird, the Kiowa chief, was a great war leader before he brought his people to the reservation. Until his untimely demise, I had no more valuable ally and friend. He provided a link between the agency and his people that was vital to keeping the peace and winning government concessions that would have otherwise been impossible. It was not an easy road for him. He was criticized by some of his people and disgruntled chiefs, but he was a great diplomat and leader, and Kiowa progress has come to a standstill because of his death."

"I think you will find Quanah possesses similar skills."

"If he will exercise his abilities in support of the cause of peace and making life better for his people, he will find me most receptive to his friendship. We will have difficult problems thrown at us from time to time, but the Comanche require a leader who can truly lead if we are to solve them together. I am anxious to meet this man."

Josh promised to personally introduce Quanah to the agent upon his arrival at the reservation.

"Bring this woman, She Who Speaks, with you. It sounds like she might be helpful in enhancing our conversation. You seem to think she is a very special person."

He had not spoken about Jael's role as the mother of his son. "I will certainly invite her, Agent Haworth."

When Josh stepped out of the agent's office, his nose and face were pelted by icy grains of sleet shooting from the sky. It appeared winter was making another visit and that his streak of good fortune with the weather had run out.

29

THE WINTER STORM had lasted off and on for a week, and it had taken another week for the weather to warm up enough to make travel sensible. The situation had improved Dr. Sturm's spirits greatly, Josh assumed because he was cashing in on rent at the rate of three dollars daily and had sold a house that had been a worthless asset in his own mind. It had taken another two weeks wandering the Staked Plains seeking Quanah's village. Most signs of activity had been obliterated by the storms, but the snow faded and eventually disappeared as they inched further south.

Cal and Wolf alternated scouting forays, and, finally, on one of his sweeps, Cal had picked up signs of frequent travel in the direction of the southern end of Palo Duro Canyon. A day later, they were overlooking a vast tipi city spread over the canyon floor.

"Well," Cal said, "we found the damn place. Now, how do we get in there and find your friend, Quanah, amongst all that conglomeration of Comanches without getting our scalps lifted? Do you speak any Comanche, Oliver?"

"No. I do not speak very good Cherokee either."

"You make a piss poor Indian."

"That's what my father said."

"I can sign pretty good," Cal said. "If they don't kill us first, maybe I can get us by until we find this She Who Speaks. Then she can talk for us."

"If you can get us to Quanah, I'm sure he'll see to our safety," Josh said.

They located a heavily-used trail that led to the canyon floor and began their descent. A few minutes later, Josh, bringing up the rear behind the packhorses, looked over his shoulder and saw three mounted Comanche warriors trailing half a dozen horses' lengths behind. So much for any notion of retreat. Word of the visitors had travelled quickly. By the time they reached the canyon floor, more than twenty-five men, women and children had gathered to greet them. They chattered excitedly, but he could detect neither welcome nor hostility in their actions. Mostly curiosity, he guessed.

He saw that Cal, who had led their party, was signing frantically, his head swiveling back and forth over the onlookers, seeking a response from someone. His efforts were futile, and Josh wondered if his younger brother had overestimated his proficiency at native sign language. The Comanche swarm parted when someone broke through the gathering, and Josh was relieved to see Quanah making his way through the crowd. He nudged his buckskin past the packhorses and other riders, and then dismounted to face the young chief.

Josh raised his hand, signaling greeting. "Hello, Chief. I come with news."

He supposed the chief did not understand anything he was saying.

"We wait for words," Quanah said.

"You speak English?"

"Me speak not much words."

"Where is She Who Speaks? She can help us."

"No She Who Speaks. Go."

Go? What did he mean? Josh had a sudden sinking feeling in his gut. "Where is Michael? Where is Flying Crow?"

"Flying Crow go."

What in blazes did he mean? Go could mean anything. Dead. Lost. Run away.

"Josh, Cal," a woman's excited voice yelled.

Josh turned to see Tabitha rushing toward him. She leaped into his arms and almost knocked him over before squeezing him nearly breathless.

"I've been watching for you for days," she said excitedly.

Cal and Wolf had dismounted now, and Cal sauntered over to his sister and tapped her on the shoulder. "Hey, Little Sis. What about your favorite brother?"

She pulled away from Josh and fell into Cal's arms and hugged him tightly. "A family reunion," she said.

Then she saw Wolf and pushed Cal aside and walked over to him, beaming, as she looked up at his face. "White Wolf, you look so . . . so well. I worried so much about you." She stepped up to him and gave him a chaste hug. "I did not know if I would ever see you again. I'm so glad you are here."

The Cherokee's face remained stoic as he nodded his greeting, but Josh saw the look in Wolf's eyes that told him Tabitha Rivers was someone he cared about very much. He did not sense that Tabby reciprocated in the same way. Then he became aware again of their audience. Many of the Comanche women were giggling at the scene that had just played out, and the men looked on with a mixture of contempt and good humor.

"Tabby," Josh said. "I asked Quanah about Jael and Michael. He said they were gone. What did he mean by that?"

Tabitha's face turned instantly glum. "I'll explain when we go to my tipi. As near as I know, they're fine. But they left."

"Left?"

"I said I would explain. Let me speak to Quanah first."

She was with Quanah for some moments while the curiosity seekers began to disperse and leave. They appeared to be conversing in a strange mix of English and Comanche that he could not make out. It seemed to work. It was like they had invented their own language.

When Tabitha returned, she said, "You will all stay with me tonight. In the morning, I will take you to Quanah and act as interpreter."

"What's for supper?" Cal asked.

"It's several hours till supper time," Tabitha replied. "But since you asked, it's roasted horse meat. That's what I have almost every night since we finished eating the dogs."

Cal looked like he was going to be sick.

30

TABITHA WARNED THE men they should stake their horses near her tipi. "White Wolf's magnificent stallion might be too tempting for some of Quanah's enemies, and they're all fair game for meat."

The men unsaddled their horses and unloaded the pack animals and carried their bedrolls and supplies into the tipi, following Tabitha's directions as to placement of their burdens. It left the lodge congested, but there was still room to maneuver and find sleeping spots when it came time.

When they had all settled in around the fire, Josh finally raised the question that had been gnawing at him. "Okay, Tabby, where did they go?"

"I don't know. It's been over two weeks now. I woke up one morning, and they were gone. She took my Henry, too. I can't believe she stole my rifle. I thought she was my friend and she up and takes off with my rifle. It really pisses me off."

Josh was miffed at his sister's sense of priorities. "She took your nephew. You're not upset about that?"

"Well, I knew you wouldn't be happy to hear it, but I know Michael's as safe with her as he would be anyplace. I love that little boy, and I know you don't want to hear this, but she is his mother. That's a fact. It has nothing to do with blood."

"You sound like you're on her side."

"I'm not on your side or her side, but I think we all ought to be on Michael's side."

"She can't run away from this. I'll find her. She doesn't know how persistent I can be."

"Stubborn is what you are. It's the Rivers family curse."

"And you're a Rivers."

"And I've got it too. Or I wouldn't be spending my winter in this godforsaken place, starving or eating horse meat." Tears came to her eyes. "I'm tired of watching these people die. I can see some dignity in dying from a bullet defending your way of life. Dying of starvation is a pitiful thing. I don't know how many babies have withered up and died, just because their mothers couldn't produce the milk to feed them. Those bastards in Washington who decided to starve the Comanche on to the reservation ought to see what I've witnessed here. Well, they've won. Most of the chiefs are following Quanah's lead now. They will go with him to the reservation. They have no choice. But remember I said this. Their troubles are not over. They will be political pawns after they get there. Politicians love dependency, and they will keep them dependent. The Comanche have had their last taste of freedom."

"I hope it's better than the picture you paint," Josh said. "I do have some encouraging news for Quanah when we meet in the morning. But after I speak with him, I'm leaving to search for Jael and Michael. Are you going to help me figure out where she took him or not?"

"I don't know where. I think she had Quanah's help. Of course, he won't understand a word if we ask him about it. Jael has worked with him on learning English all winter, and she said he understands it better than he speaks it. He's slick as a greased snake. He has very selective hearing. If you ask him a question he doesn't want to answer, he will choose not to comprehend."

"Why do you think Quanah helped her?"

"First, the two warriors . . . Scratching Turkey and Growling Bear . . . he usually sent with her on her missions to meet you were gone for several days after she left. I'd guess they escorted her part way to wherever she was going. Then Quanah informed me I could have her few remaining horses. He would have kept them if he hadn't made a commitment to Jael. It's a wonder he didn't anyway."

"Did she ever mention any town or city that interested her . . . a place she might like to see or live in? She is something of a chameleon, if you think about it. Her language skills would let her move easily in several cultures, and her coloring's such that she could pass for white or a Mexican, I suspect."

"She loved Santa Fe and talked about what she did and saw there a lot when she first came back . . . before she started to withdraw."

"What do you mean?"

"A few weeks after she returned, she started to get quiet and moody. At first, I thought she was angry at me about something, but then I decided it was about Michael. During this time, she mentioned several times she would like to go to Denver. She had never been there, of course, but she thought it would be a city with opportunity. I told her that Ham was in banking there and could probably find her a position. She quit talking about Denver after that."

"Do you think she was serious about Denver?"

"I think she wanted you to look for her in Denver."

"Me too. Where would you go?"

She thought a minute. "South. If I spoke Spanish fluently, I would move in the direction of the border. It would give me options if I decided I had to keep moving. As you said, she's a chameleon and can change her colors to fit in where she's at. She's also one of the most resourceful persons I've ever met."

Cal laughed. "Next to you, Little Sis."

Josh turned to Wolf. "Oliver, you've scouted this country. Where's her logical destination from here?"

"The closest would be Fort Concho and the little town of San Angelo growing around it. I've been there a few times. A busy place. But it doesn't seem a likely hideout for a Comanche to head for."

"But she's been shedding her Comanche skin all winter. Michael wasn't allowed to speak a word of Comanche all winter," Tabitha said. "I should have known. She was preparing for this. She had it all planned out."

"Well, she's not getting away with it," Josh said. "She can go where she damn well pleases, but I'm finding Michael, and he's coming back with me, even if I have to hog-tie him to a horse. I'm riding out right after I meet with Quanah. I'll try to be back before Sturm meets up with Quanah this spring. I don't think that will happen before late April. If I haven't found Michael, I'll be back for the peace conference and then head out again."

"Count me in," Cal said. "I'll go with you."

"I think you should stay with Tabby till this is all over. I don't want to leave her here without somebody."

"Let Oliver do that."

"I've done fine so far," Tabitha said. "I don't need a caretaker."

Josh ignored her. "Oliver, would you mind staying with Tabby?"

"I would be willing to do that, if she does not object."

Tabitha shrugged. "I'm confused by this 'Oliver' talk, but it would be fine for White Wolf to stay. I would welcome someone else who can speak English. Between us, perhaps, we can do some good for some of these people during the wait."

Wolf said, "I used the last of my paper. If I could find something to write on, I can sketch some landmarks and maps for you to use on the trail to Concho."

"I can supply that," Tabitha said.

31

THE MORNING OF Rylee's rescue, Jael had caked Rylee O'Brian's whip slashes with a salve she had concocted from ground willow bark, skunk bush and fat she had scraped from a rabbit Michael killed. She would have preferred buffalo fat and other ingredients, but she had to work with what was available. The wounds had started healing nicely over the past four days. There would always be telltale scars, but they would fade, hopefully with the girl's memory of her abuse.

This morning Jael had informed the girl she must abandon her long underwear for a time, and she and Rylee were both attired in bright peasant blouses and full cotton skirts, garments that Jael noticed were worn by many Mexican women in Santa Fe. Michael, after token resistance, donned a green shirt and a pair of cotton britches she purchased in Santa Fe. He especially hated the boots they had struggled to pull on his feet.

After they washed the breakfast plates and pans and put everything in the recently acquired wagon, Jael and the children crowded into the rear of the wagon to discuss her plans for the day. "Joseph," she said, "what is your last name?"

"Davis," Michael said. "My name is Joseph Davis. Sometimes you and aunt Rylee call me 'Joe.' Your name is Ruth. Aunt Rylee is your sister, and your mother was Mexican, and your father was Irish. His name was Daniel O'Brian. My father, Jacob, died from . . . smallpox."

"Very good." The boy seemed to enjoy the pretense. It had to be confusing for him to keep changing his name, but it was necessary to add another layer of deception, in case someone heard of missing persons bearing the names of Michael Rivers or Jael Chernik. At first, she had planned to claim Rylee as her daughter but reconsidered when she realized the girl was not more than ten years younger than herself.

"Ruth," Rylee said, "we could sell everything we have here for a lot of money. You said you lived with the Comanches for a lot of years, do you know what things are worth?"

"I have no idea. But I would like to sell everything but our saddle horses. I've tried to dispose of everything that would tie us to the Comanche. The saddles and tack that belonged to our late friends have been very convenient. We should take from the wagon only those things we foresee needing soon . . . some blankets, a few more clothes and cooking supplies. The canned beans and some of the food items, we should save. We should find lodging. We will attract attention if we stay in the wagon."

Rylee said, "I can go to the general store and walk around and check prices on things. The rifles should be worth the most. Then we should offer to sell everything in the wagon for half of what he's listing it at. The storekeeper will try to dicker, but you tell him we'll set up the wagon down the street from his place and sell the merchandise by the piece. He'll come around fast. He won't want competition, and he won't pass on the chance to double his money."

"How do you know all of this?"

"I went with Pa every place. Sometimes I helped him dicker. Mother said I was good with money and that we wouldn't have been so poor if Pa would have let me take care of it. I don't mean to speak bad about Pa. He was the kindest, gentlest man you'd ever meet, but he wasn't cut out for business."

"Very well. When we get to town, why don't you make a visit to the general store?"

"I need to buy something if I don't want to get booted out. Do you have any coins at all?"

Jael plucked her little doeskin bag from under the gun crate. She opened it and poured some of Quanah's coins in her hand. "How much do you need?"

"I'll be a jug-head. Where in blazes did you get that? Do you know how much money you're holding in your hand?"

"No, I don't remember money things very well."

"You've got two gold eagles, a double eagle and three one dollar gold pieces. That's forty-three dollars. And you've got more in the bag? Ruth, we don't have money problems. I'll take one of the dollar gold pieces and buy you a nice pocket book. A proper lady should have one. Then, if it's okay with you, I'll buy some candy for Joe and me."

"I don't suppose he's ever had candy."

"It's about time he did. One of the joyful sins of civilized folks. Think of it as a part of his education. As soon as we get to town, I'll be on my way. Be on the lookout for a livery. We'll sell the wagon and the horses we don't need. We ought to get twenty-five dollars for the team and ten dollars for each of the others. I would guess twenty for the wagon. I'll get him to throw in board for the three we keep for two weeks."

"You are making my head spin. What would I have done without you?"

"Maybe the Good Lord thought it was about time to give us both a break. Oh, I don't mean to be greedy or anything. But do I get a cut out of all this money we're going to be taking in?"

Jael thought a moment and then replied. "We are partners, I would say. Half and half."

Rylee beamed and gave that infectious smile she had started to show occasionally the last few days. Then she climbed out of the wagon bed and onto the seat. She picked up the reins and said, "Time's wasting. Let's get this wagon rolling."

32

THEY HAD ARRIVED on the outskirts of San Angelo late the previous evening and set up camp near the river, well off the main trail they had come across earlier in the day. There was a lot of traffic on the trail, civilian and military, but they had not encountered any unpleasantness, and nobody seemed curious enough to ask any questions. Mostly, they received congenial waves from other travelers, and more than once an appreciative turn of the head from a young cowboy or soldier. Jael found she didn't mind the attention all that much.

Early this morning Rylee had dressed, and, after downing a dry biscuit, had walked briskly out of the camp to find the little town's main street. A few hours later, she returned to report and dole out some licorice sticks and chunks of hard candy. "We'll save the rest for later," she said, setting her candy bag in the wagon.

Jael had been allotted a candy share of her own, and the licorice brought back memories of the years she lived in New York after her parents immigrated from Germany and before the disastrous journey west. She remembered a candy store stocked full of every sugary delight imaginable. She found the hard candies more to her liking than the licorice, but Rylee and Michael devoured it all with equal enthusiasm.

Rylee handed Jael a large leather bag with a shoulder strap and several compartments. "Not as fancy as some," she said, "but nice enough and practical. You can put your bag of coins in there. After we sell everything, I'll buy a bag to carry my share."

"Do you think we'll make some money?"

"Well, it's all profit to us. But let me go over what we've got again." She jumped in the wagon and began to rummage through the contents. "I suppose we should keep a few of the rifles we took off the renegades," she hollered. "I know I want one, and the new ones will bring us a better price."

"Yes, let's keep two and some ammunition." That way she would still have a rifle if she found a way to return the Henry to Tabitha someday. "Do you want one of their pistols? I already have one."

"No. I can handle a Winchester well enough, but an Army Colt has too much kick for me. They've got something in the general store that's just out by Colt. They call it the National Deringer pistol. It's an itty-bitty thing. It would fit snug as a bug in a pocket book. Nobody'd ever guess it was there. I'll bet I can dicker for two for the price of one. They don't seem to be selling. Out in this part of the country, there's not much call for a weapon like that. I don't think this storekeeper is much of a businessman. He's overstocked in stuff that nobody would want and understocked in things folks in west Texas might be looking for."

Jael marveled as Rylee rattled off prices she had stored in her head. It occurred to her that the young lady was to numbers as she was to languages.

Michael, who had been quiet up to this point, asked, "Mother, can I have a rifle?"

This Comanche boy had been forced to abandon the weapons of the Kwahadi, which were also tools for living, Jael thought. Why not? She and Rylee could teach him to use the firearm. "Yes, Michael, you should have a rifle."

"My name is Joseph now. But thank you, Mother. May I choose?"

"Now I am the one who is confused. Yes, Joseph. Choose one of the rifles. You may pick mine out also."

Michael climbed into the wagon with Rylee, and Jael stood there for a moment enjoying the banter between the two. They had quickly become like brother and sister, she observed. It gave her a warm feeling. And then she shuddered at the thought she was now responsible for two young lives with no more than a vague notion of where this journey was leading.

Three hours later they sat in a dirty, frame shoebox of a café, enjoying an early afternoon dinner. The steaks and baked potatoes were more than passable, and the apple pie was scrumptious. Michael, of course, had never eaten in such magnificent surroundings and was wide-eyed as he took in every nook and cranny of the cramped room. Jael had been teaching him how to use the eating utensils ever since they acquired the wagon, but he still handled his knife and fork clumsily and asked repeatedly if he could just pick up the steak and bite off the meat chunks. Jael responded with the look that only mothers can deliver in such instances.

The wagon contents had sold for just short of two hundred dollars; the guns, including those salvaged from the Comancheros, accounting for almost half of the figure. The wagon and surplus horses took in a bit over one hundred dollars. After the split with Rylee, and a few purchases at the general store, Jael figured she had about one hundred fifty dollars not counting the coins Quanah had given her. She found herself quickly learning how money was counted and what things were worth, but she had left all the haggling to Rylee, who appeared to enjoy the process.

Money would not be a problem for the short term, but where did they go from here? She was uncertain she would ever be able to put enough distance between her and Josh Rivers. She knew him to be tenacious and obsessive in pursuing any task, and she could not fault him in this instance. It saddened her to hurt him like this, and, strangely, since their shared evening in Santa Fe, she had struggled with thoughts of the comfort that seemed to come with his presence. The memory of his kiss lingered.

She shook off her melancholy. "We must find a place to stay until we decide where to go next," she announced.

"We should find a boarding house," Rylee said. "I noticed one when we I came into town earlier. It was right off main street."

Rylee leading the way, they strolled down the dusty street toward the boarding house. They had left their gear and weapons at the livery, not wanting to attract undue attention or alarm the host or hostess at the boarding house. They arrived at a two-story clapboard, white-washed house that looked quite elegant compared to most of the buildings in town. A small sign next to the door declared the establishment's name was "Grandma's House."

Before Rylee knocked, Grandma opened the door and greeted them with a wide smile, revealing perfect teeth that gleamed against the background of her tawny skin. She was a short, buxom woman pushing sixty, plump but not obese. Jael guessed she was what some called mulatto.

"Welcome, children. Do I see paying boarders at my door?"

"Yes," Jael said. "We're looking for a room. We don't know how long yet. At least two nights."

"Well, come on in. I'm Ida Jefferson. Most just call me Grandma."

The door opened into a small immaculate parlor. "Do you prefer main floor or upstairs," Grandma asked. "I've got three rooms on each floor."

"What's the cost difference?" Rylee asked.

"One dollar a night per person for two rooms upstairs. I've got one room taken with a permanent boarder. Downstairs rooms are a dollar and a half for each of you and you can have two rooms."

Rylee said, "We'll pay a total of two dollars for the three of us, and we'll just use one downstairs room."

Grandma cocked her head and eyed Rylee suspiciously, and Jael could see she was working the numbers in her head.

Grandma said, "I generally include breakfast and supper in the price, and there are three of you."

Rylee replied, "I was assuming those meals were included in my offer."

Grandma burst into laughter. "Honey, I think I've met my match. Privy's out back, but you got to furnish your own paper. Pump's just outside off the kitchen."

Jael spoke quickly, seeing Rylee was preparing to negotiate on the paper. "I'm Ruth Davis, Grandma, and this is my son, Joseph. You've been dealing with my sister, Rylee O'Brian. If you'll show us our room, we'll go to the livery and pick up our things."

"Sold it to you sight unseen, didn't I? For all you know I'm lodging you in a tipi."

"We would survive that, I'm quite certain."

33

JAEL HAD DECIDED to take her chances in San Angelo. She and Michael were accustomed to the nomadic life, but now there was another to consider. She knew Rylee was tough and resilient, but she concluded it was not in the interest of either child to be constantly on the move. She had no way of knowing what dangers lurked on the way to other destinations. At least with an Army post nearby, there was the promise of certain stability and job opportunities, perhaps, for someone skilled in words and languages. She would make her stand here and hope that Josh was looking elsewhere.

They loved staying at Grandma's. The room was spacious when compared to her former abode. Michael hated beds and slept on the floor, while Jael and Rylee shared the room's double bed. Jael found she did not share Michael's hostility to a soft straw mattress. After deciding they would stay for a time, Rylee had bargained for a monthly rate that reduced their lodging costs, and Grandma's House was now home. Jael had no memory of eating as well as they had the past few days. Grandma's flapjacks, soaked with thick maple syrup, had triggered memories again of another life that she had put on a shelf somewhere after her abduction by the Comanche. She felt no small amount of guilt over how well she was faring, however, when she thought of the tribulations her Comanche brothers and sisters were now undergoing.

Fort Concho did not fit her image of a military post. There were no more than a dozen small buildings scattered about and no fortifications to speak of. The soldiers were evidently housed in a hodgepodge of larger canvas wall tents and tiny pup tents. She sat now in a tiny reception area of the commanding officer's headquarters. The master sergeant at the desk was a handsome Negro man, probably one of the buffalo soldiers she had heard about. He had been very businesslike, but courteous, when she informed him she wanted to speak to someone about interpreting positions. He had not been encouraging until she mentioned she spoke Comanche. He had then told her to wait a moment and tapped on the officer's door.

The sergeant returned soon and said, "Colonel Grierson would be pleased to speak with you, ma'am."

Shortly, a lean, gray-haired man, with a full mustache that curved up at the tips, appeared. He stood erect and confident in a spotless uniform. "Mrs. Davis, I'm delighted to meet you." He reached for her hand and she extended it, but was surprised when the colonel bobbed his head down and brushed his lips against it softly.

"I am Colonel Benjamin Grierson, ma'am. Please join me in my office." He led her into a room that might have been twice the size of the clothes closet in her room at Grandma's House. He pulled back a captain's chair for her to sit in, and then squeezed around the simple table that served as his desk and sat down. The colonel gazed at her appraisingly, but not in an offensive manner. She supposed he did not interview many female interpreters.

"Sergeant Monroe tells me you speak Comanche."

"Yes. I do."

"How well do you speak the language?"

"Fluently."

"I see. May I ask how you came to speak the language so well?"

"I was a captive. But it is difficult for me to talk about."

The Colonel cleared his throat. "I'm sure. Well, it so happens we have a need for interpreters for Comanche prisoners who are brought to the fort. I am the new commander of the Tenth Cavalry out of Fort Concho. You may have heard them referred to as buffalo soldiers. Ah, it's because of their kinky hair, like the buffalo, you see."

"I see."

"But they are a crack fighting unit . . . the best. I'm proud to command them. Our job is to track down and bring in bands of Comanche who refuse to go to the reservation. We expect the Kwahadi to surrender soon, but it will take a year or two to collect the renegades here and there who continue to fight the inevitable. My problem is Colonel Mackenzie, who has been here temporarily, was named commander at Fort Sill and departed a week ago for his new posting, taking with him the few interpreters we had here."

"So, you might have a need for my services?"

"Do you have any problem associating with the savages? We will assure your safety, of course, but some may be belligerent."

"That would not concern me." What did concern her was that she might encounter recalcitrant Kwahadi who would recognize her. On the other hand, the white soldiers would have no idea what the prisoners were saying, and there would be no point to a Comanche warrior identifying her anyway.

"We can pay you sixty dollars a month to be available as needed. That's twice what an enlisted soldier makes."

And that would cover room and board, allowing her and Rylee to preserve their funds. Somehow, she took satisfaction in finding she was making her way quite well in the white world. "That should be satisfactory. I can tell the sergeant how to locate me, and I will come to the post whenever you summon me."

34

"I WILL MOVE my things out this afternoon and find other shelter," Wolf said, as he and Tabitha sat by the fire in her tipi. Josh and Cal had departed after Josh's meeting with Quanah that morning. He decided it would not be proper for him to share sleeping quarters with Tabitha unchaperoned.

"Nonsense. I don't want to be alone. The Kwahadi have greater concerns than the propriety of any living arrangements we have. I'm sure they would be more surprised if you moved out. We can share this tipi and behave like a proper gentleman and lady. I am certain of it."

"I must admit I am not anxious to bed down in a cave somewhere . . . if I could find one."

"Then it's settled. You will stay here. Now, tell me what became of White Wolf."

"He disappeared after he met Charles Goodnight. When I was stabbed by She Who Speaks's little savage and escaped from the village you were in at that time, Goodnight found me. He cared for me and saved my life, and I was with him for several weeks exploring the Palo Duro. He said if I was going to live in the white world I should have a proper name. He tagged me as 'Oliver' for his late partner and friend, Oliver Loving. So, Oliver Wolf was born. I was getting ready to re-join the cavalry unit when we came upon your brothers."

"Thank God you did. That's how I learned you were still alive."

"I felt very foolish when I discovered I was trying to rescue someone who didn't want to be rescued."

"It must have been very confusing, but, by the time you arrived, I felt I was no longer in danger. Jael had taken me under her wing, and Josh's connection with Quanah made me feel I was not risking my life by staying here . . . at least the Comanche wouldn't likely harm me. And the opportunity for me as a reporter and writer was something I couldn't resist. I have gathered volumes of material and buckets of ideas. Newspaper articles. A book. There are so many stories people must hear about."

"You sound like a Comanche convert."

She laughed. "I just see another point of view and have empathy for the People, as they call themselves."

"You have been with the Comanche more than six months now. Aren't you ready to go home?"

"Absolutely. A soft bed. A steak prepared at The Exchange. Apple pie. But I would not have missed this for anything. Besides, there is the connection forged with my nephew and Jael. I'm mad as hell at her for running off with Michael and my Henry, but I love her like a sister. She's one of the most remarkable persons I've ever met."

"What will Josh do if he finds her. Violence does not seem to come easily to him."

"Oh, he wouldn't harm her . . . not physically, anyway. But he will take Michael, and that will break her heart. She loves that boy. She would die for him in a minute."

"Does she love him enough to give him up?"

Tabitha did not answer immediately as she pondered his question. "Yes, she will do that if she must to spare him more pain. If she determines the battle for Michael is lost, she will disappear from his life. She knows from experience that children can suffer loss and recover and make new lives. She would allow Michael to start a new life with his father without her interference. She loves him that much."

"This is very sad."

"It is. Let's talk about something else. Tell me how you came to show up here with my brothers."

Oliver Wolf told her his story, of his ambitions as an artist and of his plans to make a new life in Santa Fe. He confessed his need to complete his mission of finding her and returning her to her people. He understood that she managed quite well for herself, but that he had been haunted by a feeling he had left a task unfinished. They paused long enough to cook and eat the last of the horse meat. He informed her he had jerky and hardtack remaining for breakfast and then he would hunt further north up the canyon for game, that it pained and saddened him to eat the flesh of horses. He felt like a cannibal.

Wolf could not recall sharing so much of himself with another person before, but Tabitha had shown a genuine interest that pierced his usual reticence and drawn out his words, sent them flowing off his tongue like a waterfall. Well after midnight, after Tabitha had fallen asleep cocooned in her buffalo robe on the opposite side of the fire, he stared into the dancing inferno of the flames. It felt right to be here with this woman, he thought. He could not envision a path that led them anyplace beyond the present, but he gave himself permission to love her anyway.

35

"I SUPPOSE THERE are some Indian trackers that can read signs like a preacher reads the Bible," Cal said. "They see things the rest of us can't see if we stick our nose right in it. Us mere mortals can't prove them right or wrong. When I scouted for the Army, I followed my gut mostly, decided where I thought somebody went and then tried to dig up something close to evidence to prove me right. My gut tells me we keep riding south and follow moving water when we can."

Josh could not argue with that. Besides, what else could they do? Quanah had done just what Tabby had predicted. He went stone deaf when Josh inquired about Jael and Michael. The war chief seemed to understand and be somewhat satisfied when Tabby, in her jumbled English and Comanche, informed him of Josh's meeting with Mackenzie. Tabby had conveyed Josh's message that he was riding out again to search for She Who Speaks and Flying Crow, and the chief had looked displeased until Josh promised his return in time to intercept Sturm and the peace emissaries to lay out the guidelines for the trek to Fort Sill.

The Rivers brothers had wandered for a week now without any sign, and Josh was getting discouraged. For all he knew the woman had taken Michael north or even east. There was nothing to prove otherwise. Perhaps, he should rethink all this, return to the Kwahadi village, meet his obligations to Quanah and then take up the search again with a fresh look at things. Cal insisted, though, that Jael had gone south and counseled patience. They would give it a few more days.

Cal raised his hand, signaling a halt, and they reined in their horses. His gaze trailed the ground in front of them and Josh realized what his younger brother was studying. Tracks, all kinds heading west. They appeared to be mostly deer, but there were a good number of prints of both shod and unshod horses scattered on the crusty prairie dirt.

"I've been seeing tracks for the past hour, but the traffic starts getting a hell of a lot heavier in front of us," Cal said.

"And you think we should see where they're going?"

"Big brother, you're starting to pick up some genuine scouting skills watching me. Yep, let's see where the party is. Ought to be some water over that way. I know a lady who likely would have figured that out."

A half hour later they came to the rim of a canyon. Josh pulled a small bundle of paper from the inside pocket of his buffalo-hide coat. He passed the sheets to Cal who shuffled through them, kept two and handed the others back to Josh. Cal dismounted and pressed the sheets side by side against his sorrel gelding's flank, lining up the sketches on the papers.

"Your friend Wolf's pretty good. Say, I got to thinking. We just went off and left Little Sis with that Cherokee. Think she'll be all right? Did you see the way he was eyeing her when he thought nobody was watching?"

"I think Tabby's shown she's not going to do anything she doesn't want to do."

"What the hell does that mean?"

"Just tell me what you see on the maps."

"This is Crazy Woman Canyon. A heavy-flowing stream fed by springs runs through it. If you stick with it going downstream, it flows into the Concho."

"Looks like a good place to spend the night. If we don't find anything to send us elsewhere, I think we should follow it to the Concho. Crazy Woman Canyon. Sounds like a place Jael might end up."

It was early afternoon on a balmy day, and they spent several hours searching for sign in the canyon. In a little clearing, not more than fifteen paces from the stream, Josh spotted scattered skeletal remains. He whistled to Cal, who was scouting further upstream. "There has been some trouble here," Josh said, as they dismounted and began walking the area. His gut went queasy at the thought of what story they might unravel.

Bones with three skulls and remnants of clothing were strewn haphazardly about the site. Vultures, coyotes and other scavengers had stripped the bones clean. "All men," Cal said. "No women or children."

Josh gave a quiet sigh of relief. "How long ago?"

"Hard to say. Two weeks. Could be a month. There's a scattering of .44 cartridge casings over there at the edge of the clearing. Somebody gunned them down. Could have been a Henry."

"Could have been a Winchester, too."

"Bet it was a Henry."

"You can't know that."

"Nope, not for sure. There was a loaded wagon here, too. Probably one of those Conestoga outfits. Look at the ruts. And take a hike over to those trees." He pointed to the south end of the campsite.

Josh followed his brother's instructions. "Whiskey. There must be twenty cases here."

Cal joined him and worked an unbroken bottle out of one of the crates. He popped the cork and took a healthy swallow. "Tastes like dog piss. But it's kind of like a worn-out whore . . . better than doing without."

Josh ignored Cal's vulgarities, not wanting to encourage him. "What do you make of this?"

"I'd guess the bones belong to Comancheros or somebody of their ilk. It was their wagon. Now it's somebody else's. It wasn't Indians. They wouldn't have tossed the firewater. Any white men that set out to steal the wagon would not have, either."

"You're not suggesting Jael massacred these men and took the wagon."

"Sounds far-fetched. But I wouldn't rule it out. There's got to be more to the story than we can figure out here."

"Let's go back up stream a bit and set up camp and get some sleep. Tomorrow we'll head south and try to find out what became of that wagon."

36

"YOU SAID YOU'VE been to Fort Concho?" Josh asked.

Cal replied, "Once, for a day stopover to resupply. It was near the end of my scouting days a few years ago. I was with the Ninth Cavalry at the time. We came in from the east and returned the same way for fifty miles before heading north. That's why I wasn't familiar with the country we just came through."

"I've been thinking we would stop there before we check out San Angelo. If Mackenzie's still at Concho, he might be of some help."

"Well, from the number of folks moving up and down the trail, I'd say we're within a few miles of something. Let's pack up and be on our way. I'm anxious to find out one way or the other if they've been down here and get started in the direction of home."

"Are you getting nervous about that red-headed spit-fire you're married to? I wouldn't blame her for getting her bristles up over you taking off with me."

"You know me. I'd rather face a Comanche war party than a mad woman out of control."

"You should have thought about that."

"If we bring Michael home, she'll forgive me right quick. I'd bet on it."

"Then let's get about doing it."

Midmorning, they led their horses into Fort Concho. A summer teaser had slipped into March, and the sun was dropping some heat on the backs of their necks. They paused at a water pump set off the side of the parade ground and watered the horses at a tank there. Each took turns on the pump handle while the other filled his canteens and then scooped the cold well water into his cupped hands to enjoy a fresh drink.

"I suppose I ought to check in at the commanding officer's headquarters and see what we can learn there."

"No," Cal said, "I've got a better idea." He nodded toward a building that sported a crudely printed sign that said "Quartermaster." "See that soldier on the porch with his foot propped up on a bucket and the crutch leaning against the hitching post? Looks like he's got a banged-up foot or leg and probably lonesome for some company. Better yet, he's a first sergeant. If you want to know what's happening on the post, don't ask a damn general. Talk to one of the sergeants."

"Okay by me."

"Let me get him started. You start your law wrangler talk, and you'll freeze his lips."

Josh decided to trust Cal's judgment.

From the instant Cal mentioned the solder's presence, Josh noticed that the sergeant's eyes were fixed on them. He was a stockily-built man, probably late forties, Josh figured, with a brushy, but carefully trimmed mustache. The man squinted his eyes against the sun's glare and tugged the bill of his Army cap down on his forehead as they led the horses across the parade ground. As they drew nearer, they had his full attention. They stopped in front of the boardwalk and tied their mounts and the packhorse to the hitching post.

"Howdy, sergeant," Cal said. "Shade you've got over here is mighty welcome today."

"If you say so."

So much for Cal's country charm, Josh thought.

Undaunted, Cal continued. "Looks like you're laid up a mite. Comanche?"

"Horse. Not that it's any of your concern."

"Horse. Got thrown?"

"Hell, no. Stepped on my damn foot. Not much glory in that for a horse soldier. Now why don't you state your business? You didn't hike over here for no social call."

"No need to get testy, sergeant. I'm Cal Rivers. I used to scout for General Mackenzie."

Not entirely false, Josh guessed. His brother had never met Mackenzie before the journey to Fort Sill, but he had scouted for officers under the general's command.

"This here's my brother, Josh," Cal said.

"He got a tongue?"

"Oh, yes. A silver one when he gets it started. He just gets emotional. We're looking for his lady friend. She took off after a fuss a while back. And we just want to make sure nothing awful happened to her."

Josh decided not to let Cal bury them with unnecessary lies. "Actually, I wouldn't call the woman a lady friend. More of an acquaintance. She ran off with my son. She can do what she pleases. I just want to pick up my son and head back to Santa Fe."

The sergeant suddenly seemed interested. Perhaps, he needed some adventure brought into his day. "Don't see many women on this post. A few civilian employees. What does she look like?"

Josh thought a moment. "She would turn a man's eye. Early twenties. Slender and willowy. Dark eyes and hair. Might look part Mexican but she's not. Doesn't smile much, but when she does, she's got a dimple on her right cheek."

"A dimple on her cheek. Sounds like you've seen her up close."

Josh felt a bit silly about the dimple, but it was something he had found endearing the night they dined. "She's smart as a whip and has some skills we thought might be useful to the Army. Is General Mackenzie still on the post? We're good friends. I'm sure he would help me out. He told me he was assuming command at Fort Sill soon."

The name dropping seemed to work. "The general rode out a good week ago. You're a friend of his, you say?"

"I like to think so. We're working together on bringing the last of the Comanche in. I'll be going back to Fort Sill before I return to Santa Fe with my son. I'll put in a good word for you with the general. What's your name, sergeant?"

"Culver. Sergeant Anson Culver. Give the general my regards. He might remember me."

"I'll do that." He decided not to press but, instead, to give the sergeant a chance to come around on his own. Josh had a feeling the man knew something.

His patience was soon rewarded. "I think I've seen the woman you're looking for. Her name's Ruth something. She works for Colonel Grierson. He commands the Tenth. Buffalo soldiers. She speaks Comanche, they say. Interprets when they bring in some renegades. Talks some Mexican, too, they say. And she's a lot more than pretty. There ain't a soldier on the post wouldn't give a month's pay to just take her to supper. Don't dress like a lady really. Wears britches and a plaid shirt when she's doing her work here. But I don't suppose it would do for a woman to show up in a ball gown to palaver with savages. No denying she's a woman no matter what she wears."

"Is she here now?"

"Nope. I'd have seen her if she was. She only shows up when the colonel sends for her."

"Any ideas where she lives."

"Yup. A place called Grandma's House. I heard this from one of the darky privates what went to fetch her for the colonel."

"Grandma's House?"

"Boarding house. Right on main street. A block south of Jeb's Livery. The place is as nice as it gets in this part of the country, they tell me."

"Know anything about a boy? He'd be nearing seven years old."

"Nope."

"Well, sergeant, you've been very helpful. We truly appreciate the information."

"Just give my regards to the general."

37

JOSH AND CAL decided to stay out of San Angelo until after sundown and set up camp near the river a mile out. As the sun dipped over the horizon, they mounted their horses and rode into town. They stopped at the livery and found a Mexican boy not more than thirteen years old minding shop. Josh told the boy they might be leaving later in the evening but paid for a full day's care and gave the boy a few extra coins for graining and giving the horses some special attention. His only words were "gracias" accompanied by broad smiles, but Josh had a hunch the boy understood English quite well because he responded promptly to every request.

The Rivers brothers strolled through the stable, making some pretense of checking the accommodations for the animals, but, in fact, they were looking over other lodgers. When they left the building, Cal commented, "Two unshod critters."

"Probably, Jael's and Michael's."

"Do you have a plan?"

"I'm open to ideas. I think we've got to move tonight. That sergeant we talked to is bound to pass the word along that we're here, and between an Army post and a small town, Jael will get word by tomorrow if she hasn't already. Anyway, she apparently hasn't left yet."

"I don't think you can just break into the boarding house, make a search and drag Michael out. Somebody's apt to start shooting," Cal said.

"I think we go to the door and knock and say we're friends of Ruth and would like to visit with her. We don't know the last name she goes by, so that's the best we can do."

"You really think two men show up at the door and ask to see a lady, that ain't going to make somebody suspicious?"

"I suppose you're right. Maybe I'd better do the door myself."

"And then what happens?"

"I don't know. I guess I just play it by ear."

"That's a hell of a plan alright. I pity your clients if you don't plot out your court cases better than this."

"I told you I was open to ideas. If you've got something better, speak up."

"As a matter of fact, I don't. But Pop always called you the thinker."

They strolled down the dirt street in silence, Josh deciding that his conversation with Cal was going nowhere fruitful. They stood outside the imposing frame structure, studying what Josh thought of as the fortifications. The soft glow of lamplights filtered through most of the downstairs windows, but the upstairs was evidently unoccupied, at least during the early evening.

"Why don't we get a couple of rooms for the night?" Josh said. "That would get us in the door."

"I wouldn't quarrel with that. I'm ready for a real bed."

"Well, we might not stay here, but this would give us a chance to check out the place and find out where Michael's at."

"I still don't know what we do if we find him. I ain't interested in shooting anybody, or getting shot, either, for that matter."

"We're not going to shoot anybody."

"Please tell me we're not going to get shot, either."

"Highly unlikely, I'd say."

"Damned lawyers. Always using the weasel words."

"Let's get this done," Josh said, walking deliberately toward the door.

He tapped softly on the door and waited. Shortly, a dusky woman with a welcoming smile opened the door. "Good evening, gentlemen. May I help you?"

Josh removed his hat, "I hope so, ma'am. We're looking for rooms, preferably two, but we can double up if necessary."

She opened the door wider. "I just happen to have two upstairs rooms available. I'm Ida Jefferson, but everybody calls me Grandma."

As he and Cal stepped inside, Josh decided to opt for the truth. "I'm Josh Rivers, Grandma, and this is my brother, Cal." He looked around the parlor they had entered and saw a lanky girl with sable hair sitting on a sofa at the far end of the room, her eyes fastened on a book. He found it interesting that the entire wall of the room was lined with books.

Grandma picked up a kerosene lantern and turned up the flame. "Follow me upstairs, gentlemen, and I'll show you the rooms."

The rooms were immaculate and inviting, a welcome contrast from most Josh had encountered in his travels. "Very nice," he said. "We'll take them." He dug in his pocket and produced two silver dollars, thinking that the woman should do well at these prices, but a clean place to spend a night was a rarity on the plains and worth a hefty premium to many travelers.

Accepting the dollars, Grandma said, "You missed supper, but this includes breakfast. There's coffee in the kitchen just off the parlor, and there is chocolate cake you can help yourselves to after you get settled in. I suppose you'll need to go get your things."

Their "things," of course, had been left at their campsite with the packhorse. "Uh, we left our clothing at the livery. We'll probably just leave it there tonight. We just need a place to get a good night's sleep. We'll take you up on the coffee and cake in a bit, though."

She lifted her brows, indicating she saw a little strangeness in their behavior, but, after lighting the lamps in the rooms, she went back downstairs without comment.

"Now what?" Cal asked.

"I think chocolate cake and coffee sounds good while we get our bearings."

When they passed through the parlor, Josh noticed the girl had disappeared. She and her mother or other relative were probably occupants of one of the rooms. He wished he had seen which one she entered, so he could eliminate one of the possibilities. They found coffee cups, small plates and knives and forks on the kitchen table next to a coffee pot and the remains of a chocolate cake in a pan. The brothers sat down at the table and helped themselves to the bounty. Josh enjoyed a slice of the rich cake, and Cal helped himself to two. Josh couldn't remember when he had tasted coffee as good. They ate silently, listening for activity in the parlor or the hallway off the apparent bedrooms. Afterward, they put the cups and dishes in a big pan on a small counter that held a few other dirty cups.

They re-entered the parlor. Josh was reluctant to start a room search until he had a chance to devise a strategy, so he seated himself on the sofa, and Cal followed his cue. "We can't sit here all night," Cal mumbled, his voice barely above a whisper.

"We won't. In a few minutes, we'll start knocking on some doors."

That turned out to be unnecessary. Suddenly, a stunningly beautiful woman wearing a simple gingham dress appeared from the hallway entrance at the opposite end of the room. Josh started to rise, but Jael snapped, "Sit down, Josh, and don't say a word."

He complied. Jael took a rocking chair across from the sofa, and then the girl who had occupied his seat a half hour earlier, stepped from the hallway with a Winchester pointed at him. She looked like she could use it. He caught a glimpse of Michael peaking around the corner with wide eyes. But the parade was not finished. Now Grandma joined the group with a hefty Colt Peacemaker in one hand and steadying her wrist with the other.

"What's this all about, Jael? You don't need a gun with me."

"Listen, Mister Whoever You Are," Grandma interrupted, "Rylee said you are Comancheros who followed them here. You sons of bitches aren't taking Rylee again and you're not touching Ruth or Joe either. I want you the hell out of my place. I'll be talking to the Army about you first thing in the morning. You'd better get moving out of San Angelo fast."

Josh said, "That girl's lying. I don't know why. I never saw her before tonight. And I sure don't know anybody named Ruth or Joe. This lady sitting across from me is Jael Chernik, and the boy you call Joe is my son, Michael."

He saw a flash of uncertainty in the woman's eyes, but she held her weapon steady.

"Shall I shoot them, Ruth? It's the only way to be rid of them," the girl said.

He could see that the girl was dead serious. "And you'll hang for it, young lady. Texas doesn't care how old you are when it comes to a hanging offense."

Grandma said, "You say the word, Ruth. We can bury them out behind the privy. Nobody'll ever know. I'll take out the greasy blond one."

Cal broke his silence. "Now look here. I just came along to keep my brother company. I'm not looking for trouble."

"We would have to kill them both," Rylee said. She turned to Jael. "What do you say, Ruth? We can have this over in a minute."

"You people are insane. All of you," Josh snapped.

Jael said, "Shut up, Josh. I am going to tell you the way it is going to be." She looked at her two defenders. "Grandma . . . Rylee. Put your guns down. Nobody's getting killed tonight."

Rylee and Grandma slowly lowered their guns.

Jael leaned back in the rocker, strangely calm and relaxed, Josh thought, not behaving at all like a woman on the run. Her dark eyes fixed on his. "I knew you would find us. I was not thinking clearly until we were about half way to San Angelo. I have been considering what I would do when this happened. I will run no more. Quanah needs my help during the final days of freedom, and I will return with you and do what I can. I will prepare Flying Crow . . . Michael for what is to be. You must get to know each other."

Jael looked at Rylee for some moments before she spoke. "Rylee, I have come to love you as my sister, but you must choose by morning. You may come with me to join the Comanche on the dismal trail, or you may stay with Grandma. You have money of your own now, and I am confident she would make a place for you here until you decide what comes next in your life."

Grandma said, "I don't understand most of this, but Rylee will have a home with me as long as she wants."

Rylee remained silent, but big tears rolled slowly down her cheeks.

Jael turned back to Josh. "There. You have won. You need not post a guard outside our door, but you may if you wish. I will explain all this to Grandma after everyone retires. I must also write a letter of resignation for the colonel. We will all have breakfast with Grandma in the morning and then Michael and I will accompany you as your prisoners."

If this was victory, Josh thought, it was certainly a bitter one, and he felt no sense of jubilation.

38

J AEL FELT LIKE a fool and seethed at the wasted time resulting from their so-called escape. On the other hand, she decided, the journey had left her with a financial stake. She was learning quickly that money could not buy her son or any other real joy, but it could give a person choices.

She took comfort in Rylee's presence as they rode their ponies at a trot well behind the Rivers brothers and Michael. She was sorry to see the disappointed look on Ida Jefferson's face when Rylee announced she would be riding out with Jael, but she had been relieved to learn she would not be left entirely without family whatever happened.

Josh had insisted Michael ride near him, and Jael had instructed the boy to do so. She knew that she was being petty, but she was not disappointed to note the absence of any animated dialogue between father and son. A day and a half out, and she had exchanged no more than a few words with Josh herself. The relationship between them was tense and wary. He had mentioned this morning they would be setting up camp at a place called Crazy Woman Canyon tonight and added the comment, "You might not know the place by that name, but I have a hunch you've been there."

She had not commented, but she knew where they were now on the Concho River, and the travel time that remained before sunset. Damn right she had visited the place and let him make of it what he wanted.

"Have you decided what to do about Michael?" Rylee asked when the horses slowed down to a walk as they moved away from the river.

"Yes."

"Well, what are you going to do?"

"Let him go."

"You can't mean that. He is your son," she said in a voice that sounded like she was about to burst into tears.

"I am nothing under the white man's law. I am a woman who held him in captivity. When we reach the reservation, he becomes Josh's son. I cannot control this. Now that Josh has found him, he will not let go."

"But Michael's the brother I lost, and I don't care what the law says. You are his mother. They didn't take our guns. We can kill them."

"We probably could, but we will not. We have both seen our families murdered. I have lived among the People where killing has been a way of life. I lost Michael's Comanche father to the white man's guns. I will kill to defend and protect those I love, but this is not the same. Josh would never harm Michael. In time Michael will learn to love him and the Rivers family. I have thought about this. I was about your age when the Comanche killed my parents and abducted me, and I hated them and feared them in those first weeks, and then, day by day, the Kwahadi became my family, and I came to love them. I think of myself as Comanche. A time will come when I am only a hazy memory. And then he will forget me."

"How can you say this so calmly?"

"I do not feel calm inside. My heart cries, but I know what I must do."

"And what do we do?"

"I told Tabitha I would like to go to Denver when I thought I could use her to misdirect Josh. Of course, I should have known better. I have never been skilled at deceit. I as much as told her where to look for me. But I thought we might go to Denver. We have some money. Together we could start a business there."

"I would do that with you, but only if we must."

That evening the travelers camped in Crazy Woman Canyon, downstream from where Jael had come upon Rylee and the Comancheros. They ate well. The two pack-horses carried ample food supplies, and they enjoyed fat slices of bacon Josh had fried in a big skillet and biscuits Cal and Jael had baked in a Dutch oven. Josh had also picked up a jar of wild strawberry jam at the general store in San Angelo, and Michael spooned generous helpings on his biscuits.

Jael noticed that Michael said little to Josh, but he was not hostile either. The first day on the trail, she thought Josh had tried too hard to make awkward conversation with the boy, but today he had evidently gained the wisdom not to press and to let the boy come around in his own time. It must be difficult, she conceded, to finally find your lost child and be unable to hug him and say what you truly feel without frightening him or pushing him away. Patience, Josh.

Darkness dropped quickly on the campsite, but there was not much night chill, so they allowed the fire to burn down to red hot embers. There was no conversation beyond Josh and Cal, who sat on the opposite side of the fire pit discussing the next day's plans.

Then, Josh abruptly turned to her and asked, "Was I right? You have been to this canyon before?"

"Yes."

"Did you see the dead bodies?"

"I did." He was obviously curious, but she was not up to dealing with his questions, and he apparently sensed her mood and decided not to press the issue.

Rylee, on the other hand, responded, "You should know that Jael saved me from bring defiled and killed by Comancheros where you saw the bodies. Those men had killed my family and were going to sell me on the border. I will not speak of it further, but that is how I came to be with her and Michael."

"That's fine, young lady. You owe me no explanation. Whatever happened, for your sake I'm glad Jael came along. This is really none of my business. My mind is just boggled by all that's happened to put us all together around this fire tonight."

Josh got up and walked slowly over to his bedroll. After a few moments, Cal said, "Goodnight folks," and followed his brother.

Several hours later, Jael awakened and saw Josh sitting alone by the fire he had built up. His eyes were fixed on the cocoon of blankets where Michael had burrowed in for the night only a few feet away from her. The fire cast a soft glow on Josh's face, and she could make out his features clearly and see the tears streaming down his cheeks. At that instant, she suddenly grasped the pain he had endured and began to see their conflict through his eyes. Michael had been in her care these five years because Comanche warriors had murdered, and no doubt raped, Josh's wife and mother. Michael had been abducted by the warriors, taken by force from the family of his birth, much as she once had. Yes, she had taken him in as her own, but he was a stolen soul, and she had known that. Her claim was an emotional one, but she had no moral or legal right to keep this boy from his father. This war between her and Josh, like most wars, was one that should have never been.

39

THE BABY'S EYES were sunk deep into his skull, filmy and lifeless. His frail, emaciated body lay limp in Tabitha's arms. His mother, Dove, lay on a robe nearby, her young body frail and shriveled as an ancient woman's. Death was coming soon for Dove, and Tabitha suspected it would be welcome. Starvation offered a cruel and merciless path to life's end.

The baby was near death, also. It was all very simple. The mother starved and could not produce the life-sustaining milk, so the baby starved. There were no wet nurses in the village. A woman who found food, consumed barely enough to survive, and could barely suckle her own child. She was not faulted by others for tending to her own.

Oliver—she had to constantly remind herself that was his name now—sat next to the baby's mother, who was delirious now, mumbling words that neither could understand. He held her hand gently and occasionally uttered in Cherokee what Tabitha took, from the tone of his voice, to be words of assurance. Dove would have no idea what he was saying either, but, perhaps, Oliver felt his strange language would be less threatening than a voice speaking in English. The husband and father, Rides Horses, was not in the village, having departed a week earlier on a hunt to retrieve food for his family. Some speculated he had been killed or captured by the soldiers. Tabitha wondered if they would ever know.

When life finally escaped from the embattled bodies of mother and child, Oliver would anchor the mother on the back of a horse and carry the baby in one arm, as he rode his magnificent stallion deeper into the canyon, where he would find a cave or fissure in the rocky wall. There, he would place the baby in the mother's arms and cover them with stones to protect their flesh from the scavengers. He had tended to the internment of a half dozen suckling babies or small children and as many old people since his arrival. It seemed that the Kwahadi and their friends had conceded to this tall, strong Cherokee the role of village undertaker.

Mother and baby son did die as expected, within minutes of each other, and Oliver silently carried out his self-assigned, somber task. It was dark when he returned to the tipi they had shared for nearly two weeks now. Tabitha had gathered more wood, but that, too, was becoming scarce, and they had to ration it carefully. They roasted the two legs of a scrawny rabbit—it seemed the rabbits had endured a difficult winter, too—Oliver had shot earlier in the day. The remainder they had given to a woman and her two hungry children.

Tabitha and Oliver sat facing each other, staring at the few remaining embers in the fire pit, which were quickly crumbling into black ash. For the first time since her capture, she was having doubts about the wisdom of her decision to stay with the Comanche. The last few months had emotionally drained her, and she could see nothing but gloom for the days ahead. For a fleeting moment, she considered asking Oliver Wolf to lead her back to Santa Fe. She had enough material for stories to keep her writing for years, and she could do it in a comfortable house and with a full belly. The thought passed quickly, however. She was given to obsessions and the story of the Comanche's last days held her in its clutches. Only death would block her from being there when Quanah's Kwahadi and their allies arrived at Fort Sill.

Tabitha looked up and saw that Oliver's dark eyes were studying her. Strangely, it did not unnerve her in the least. They had grown nearly as intimate as husband and wife in their days together, except in the carnal ways. She knew it would take little encouragement for him to leap that final hurdle, and she had been tempted to signal her interest more than once. But it was a bridge she was determined not to cross, not now, perhaps, never. The road map she had charted for her life did not include a serious romance, and she did not think a casual affair was possible between them.

The memory of David, the man she almost married, floated through her mind. They had fallen in love while she was in school in Denver. He was a handsome young physician, who had swept her off her feet. She had surrendered her virginity to him without regret, and they had planned to announce their engagement as soon as he asked Pop's permission, a concession to the old rancher's ego. They would have been married with or without his approval, but David had cut his hand picking up a broken bottle from the street while they were walking. A simple wound, requiring only three stitches. A month later, he was dead from the resulting infection. No, she was far from ready for that type of commitment again, and she was not going to risk pregnancy or any other potential complications by surrendering to her lust for this man. Rationality and common sense were Tabitha Rivers's credos.

She was curious about him, though. Oliver was probably nearly ten years older than her twenty-two. Many men seemed reluctant to talk about their war experiences, but Oliver said little about the before and after, either. She wanted to know more about him, and a good reporter should be able to find out.

"I babble on about my family all the time, but you never talk about yours. Are your parents living?" she asked.

"My mother lives in eastern Arkansas near my brother and his family. Yankees killed my father at the Battle of Sharpsburg . . . the Union called it the Battle of Antietam. He was a full colonel with General A. P. Hill's division. They moved up from Harpers Ferry to support Lee, so he could at least make a dignified pullback from his failed invasion of Maryland. Dad was left behind. We don't know where he's buried. That was in '62, so it was early in the war. He was half-Scottish and a career soldier. His parents were Georgians . . . his mother was Georgia Cherokee. That was before the Trail of Tears. I keep thinking we're reliving that history now."

"Yes. I understand."

"That's one reason so many Cherokee fought with the Confederacy. The Indian Removal Act of 1830 forced the Cherokee from their lands throughout the south and sent them on the tragic trek to a reservation in eastern Oklahoma. And our people were at peace with the whites. Fortunately, many of the Cherokee were mixed blood and educated and acquired farms and blended with society off the reservation, and the federal government left them alone, as long as there were no tribal lands to steal."

"You sound so matter-of-fact. You say this with only a tinge of bitterness."

"It is done. The clock cannot be turned back. I have seen too many men make nothing of their lives because of wallowing in self-pity over some injustice done to them or their ancestors. It may have happened in Europe or China or Africa, but if you search far enough back, probably every soul in America has an ancestor who was the victim of some injustice. Many came here to escape it. Unfortunately, many have forgotten."

"I have never heard you speak like this. You are not only an artist; you are a philosopher."

Wolf shrugged. "Let us say I have opinions, but I am very cautious about who I express them to."

"And you have a brother? Are you close?"

"No." His voice was firm, and a grim look settled on his face.

"I see."

"I was engaged to a young woman. While I was off to war, my brother married her. We are twins. In all fairness, they had not heard from me for so long they convinced themselves I was dead. They have three children. I do not hate them, and I wish them well, but such things do not make for closeness. Another reason I headed west."

She decided to shift the direction of the conversation. "You have done good work here, but I want you to know that I will be fine if you must return to Santa Fe. The Comanche will not harm me."

"I have promised to check on repairs and alterations to a property your brother purchased for his law firm near Fort Sill, and I have a project at the Teatro Santa Fe I must complete, so I expect to leave soon. But I will be here until your brother returns."

"You are working for Jessica Chandler?" Tabitha adored Jessica, but the thought of the actress and theater manager in daily contact with Oliver struck her with a wave of unexplainable jealousy. She tried to wipe from her fertile mind the image of a naked Oliver romping in a cozy bed with Jessica. She just knew Jessica would not be able to keep her hands off this elite specimen of a man. And she doubted Oliver could resist. All of her will power almost disappeared.

"Yes, Jessica has been very kind to me."

I'll bet she has, Tabitha thought, but, instead, she said, "Jessica's a very kind woman. I'm very tired tonight. I think I'm going to turn in."

40

AL GRUNTED AND slumped over in his saddle when the arrow burrowed into his back. Josh rode up to his brother's side, casting his eyes about as he tried to locate the source of the assault. "Can you hang on?" he asked.

"For now. Where are the bastards?"

The question was answered when not more than a dozen Comanche warriors rose like apparitions from the sagebrush and tall grass that blanketed the flat prairie. The warriors, most with arrows nocked, were not more than fifty feet distant and surrounded Josh's party on all sides. They walked slowly and silently toward the riders.

Jael nudged her mare forward. "Don't fire. Let me speak to them." She turned her horse away and headed toward a taller warrior who wore a beat-up cavalry officer's hat and seemed to be the leader of the assailants.

Josh turned to Michael, who had been ordered by Jael to remain with Josh the past several days. They had finally started talking some, albeit awkwardly. "Are the warriors Kwahadi?" Josh asked.

"Yes, but they do not like Quanah. They say his white blood now rules his brain. The one in the soldier's hat is Fights Many. He says he will not take the trail to the reservation."

Suddenly, Jael began screaming at the warriors in Comanche. They stopped in their tracks, and she obviously had their attention. Josh had no idea what she was saying, but she spoke with ferocity and authority. "What is your mother saying?" he asked, realizing at that moment he had been referring to Jael as Michael's mother ever since they departed San Angelo when speaking to the boy. But that's who she was, as far as Michael was concerned.

"She tells the warriors to go away. She says if they attack, our guns will kill many of them . . . maybe all. And if they harm us any more, Quanah will have their man parts cut off and fed to the dogs. My mother is very angry."

Fights Many screamed back at Jael and waved his fist at her, but he whirled and started walking away at a fast pace. The others moved back and veered off to follow him, presumably to horses that were hidden in a nearby draw or somewhere else out of sight.

Josh turned his attention to Cal. His brother clung to his sorrel gelding, but his head rested on the horse's neck. The arrow had entered his rib area it appeared, and the back of his shirt was blood-soaked. Josh dismounted and handed Buck's reins to Michael. He reached up to assist Cal down from his own horse, when Cal fainted dead away and dropped off his mount and into Josh's arms, sending them both crashing to the ground with Cal landing on top.

By this time Jael had returned, and she and Rylee tugged Cal off Josh. She immediately took charge. "At least he fell facedown and didn't cause more damage with the arrow," she remarked. "Find a blanket from his bedroll, and we will slide him onto it. I will need a canteen, so I can clean the wound. Rylee, please get the penknife from my pocketbook. There should be a tweezers there somewhere, too."

Josh removed Cal's bedroll from behind the sorrel's saddle and rolled it out and removed a wool blanket. He saw Rylee fishing in Jael's big pocketbook for the knife. He had found it comical to see the ladies with the pocketbooks lashed onto their saddlebags in this rugged country, but it seemed Jael was adapting to civilization quickly. Of course, there seemed to be a practical side, for the things appeared bottomless, yielding up infinite treasures. Once he had observed Jael plucking out a small pistol for examination.

Soon they had Cal stretched out on the blanket. Jael sliced Cal's shirt from his back and with deft fingers probed the wound, which did not seem to be bleeding so profusely now. "I wish we had some whiskey. My father used it frequently in his medical practice, both for sedation and cleaning wounds."

"Let me check," Josh said. He walked back to the two packhorses Rylee had staked out and began rummaging through the bundles on the animal he and Cal shared. Shortly, he felt the unmistakable smooth glass of a whiskey bottle. He clasped it by its neck and yanked it out. It was one of the Comanchero bottles Cal had confiscated. He returned to Jael with the bottle in hand. "Here's your whiskey. I won't guarantee the quality."

"Your brother's?" she asked, taking the whiskey bottle and setting it down next to her.

"Yes, but I imagine you know where he got the stuff. It seemed to be the only thing you left behind."

She rolled her eyes, and the dimple in her cheek appeared as she returned the slightest of smiles. "I can remove this. It is a narrow arrowhead. The barbs are lodged just under his skin." She turned to Rylee, who was on her knees beside Jael, watching intently. "Rylee, I must make some bandages. Would you fetch the cotton shirt I purchased for Michael?"

When Rylee returned, Jael said, "This will only take a few minutes, but I suspect the pain will wake him. And we must keep him still. Josh, you should place your hands on his shoulders and hold him down. Michael, you sit down on his bottom, and Rylee, I want you to pull as hard as you can on his ankles."

As soon as they had Cal anchored, Jael pulled open the smaller of the knife's two blades, and Josh could see it had been honed to razor sharpness. She bent over Cal and made two quick slashes in the flesh covering his ribs. In the same instant Cal let loose with a howl that would have shamed a wolf, and Josh could feel his brother's powerful shoulders lifting, as he tried to resist Josh's pressure. They had him pinned for the moment, though, and Cal relaxed and seemingly surrendered.

Jael pulled on the arrow, and it slipped out easily. Cal moaned again and she poured whiskey on the wound. Cal reacted and yelled, "Damn it. Let go of me."

"Release him," Jael said. By this time, they had no choice. Cal's captors were trying to wrestle down a raging bull.

When Cal was finally sitting upright, Jael sliced and tore Michael's new shirt into strips, tying some of the narrow strips together before she wrapped it around his torso and anchored a crude bandage over the seeping wound.

Cal sat on the blanket for a spell, and Jael knelt nearby, studying him with professional interest. Josh and the youngsters stood nearby.

"Hurts like hell," Cal complained. "Where did those Comanche come from . . . and why?"

"We rode right into the jaws of their trap," Josh said. "You're some Indian scout."

"I wasn't expecting nothing. We can't be more than five miles from the Kwahadi village. What was that all about? By rights we all ought to be scalped and dead by now."

"Jael chased them off," Josh said, "while you were snoozing on your horse."

Cal furrowed his brow. "This is getting more confusing. I thought the last of the Comanche were on the trail to peace."

Jael interrupted. "Most of the Kwahadi and the Kiowa at our village will follow Quanah. Even now Isa-tai has decided to be a great peacemaker. But there are some for whom the wars are not finished. Fights Many has a small band of followers who will fight on. There are others who refuse to follow Fights Many who will split off into their own bands and will refuse to go to the reservation. Quanah will not force them to come. That is the Comanche way. Freedom is not a word; it is a way of life. You are with the People because you choose to be. It is not unusual for small groups to split off and form another band or to begin living with a different large band."

"But why attack us?" Cal asked.

"They were restless to send a message that they will not be a party to any surrender. They did not recognize me in these canvas riding britches and baggy flannel shirt. Michael was dressed as a white boy. They thought we were a party of foolish whites who had stumbled accidentally into Comancheria. We still enjoy Quanah's protection. Fights Many fears Quanah nearly as much as he hates him. He did not want to provoke the war chief. He felt compelled to threaten me and make noise to save face, but my only concern was to be certain he recognized me before they swarmed us."

"Well," Cal said, "for my part they sure didn't see you soon enough."

"I am sorry for that, but your wound should heal quickly. It will be painful for several weeks, because the arrow point struck between two ribs, but the wound was not terribly deep. If you can ride the short distance to the village, I will make a poultice that will hurry the healing and ease the pain."

"If you'll give me what's left in the whiskey bottle, I can take care of the pain myself."

"No, the whiskey bottle will go with my things, in case we need it for further treatment of your wound. I am also going to ask Josh to check your belongings and dispose of any other spirits. You are not going to take any liquor into a Comanche village. This might be a good time for you to stop drinking."

Josh could see that his brother was not taking to the directives issued by a female. Perhaps it reminded him too much of home.

"What are you," Cal asked, "one of them temperance ladies that takes axes to saloons?"

"I do not know what you mean by 'temperance ladies.' I am just telling you that we'll leave you for buzzard food if you try to take your spirits into a Kwahadi village."

41

WORD SPREAD LIKE a prairie fire as Josh and Jael approached the village some distance ahead of their companions. They had moved the horses at a walk, in deference to Cal's wound. As they descended into the canyon, Jael had abandoned her nursing watch to Rylee and took the lead, thinking her Comanche language skills might be useful if they encountered other hostility from those in the encampment.

Her concerns were unfounded, however. She encountered only mild curiosity reflected in the dull and sunken eyes of most of the inhabitants who gathered on the outer edges of the village. Two broke free from the crowd and raced toward them. It gave Jael a warm feeling when she saw her friend, Tabitha, approaching. At least she hoped they were still friends. She and Josh both dismounted and led their horses toward the greeters.

Jael recognized the other as Oliver Wolf, the handsome Cherokee, who trailed at a trot behind Tabitha.

Tabitha ran first into her brother's arms. She clung to him for some moments and kissed him on the cheek before she turned to Jael and gave her a warm hug. "I'm so glad you're back," she said.

"I had to return your rifle. Sorry."

"Who cares about that damned Henry? Well, I guess I do. You'd better not be showing your face here without it."

"It's on the pack horse. I turned it into a nice profit, by the way."

"Now that sounds interesting. Tell me about it."

"It is a long story. I will tell you another time if you promise not to tell your brother. I take a sadistic pleasure in keeping him in the dark about such things. It is better if he does not know for certain what I am capable of."

"Speaking of brothers. I see Cal and Michael coming along, but they're moving like snails. And there's somebody else. A young woman?"

"Yes, and she's part of the story. But Cal's injured. Do not be concerned. He will be fine, but Fights Many and some of his malcontents attacked us this morning. Cal took an arrow in his ribs. I have removed it and will treat the wound further when we get him settled in the tipi.

He will have some discomfort but not nearly so much as he will tell you. He is not what you would call stoic about such things."

"No, Cal would be the least stoic of the Rivers clan. Now, Josh is stoic. Never know what he's thinking about."

Removing Cal from his horse was an easy task this time. The muscular Wolf probably could have carried Cal alone, Jael thought, but with Josh's assistance and Cal able now to support himself some on his own legs, he was easily maneuvered into the tipi where his bedroll had been spread out atop a buffalo robe.

Fortunately, Jael always kept a collection of her powders in small urns, and they had been undisturbed during her absence. She quickly mixed a poultice and applied it to Cal's gaping wound. He groaned when she pressed some of her medication into the depths of the laceration, but he admitted soon after that the pain had abated noticeably.

After treating Cal, she asked Josh to accompany her to visit Quanah. She had gold coins to return, and she had decided she would see the trek to the reservation through before she and Rylee headed to Denver. Also, she was determined during her long "goodbye" to ease Michael into the changes that were coming to his life.

Quanah seemed pleased to see She Who Speaks. As they sat down in the war chief's lodge, she tossed him the doeskin bag of gold coins he had sent with her. "These belong to you, Chief," she said in Comanche. "I did not need them, but I thank you for your generosity. Now, I am once again at your service."

They spoke at some length, Quanah politely expressing his pleasure at her return and his sadness that her escape had been aborted. She sensed great relief, however, that she would be available to act as his interpreter with the whites in the days ahead, and she felt no small amount of guilt at her foolish desertion of the man who had given her unprecedented status for a woman in his band. She vowed to make it up to him. She realized it would be considered rude for her and Quanah to carry on such a lengthy dialogue in their common language with another present who did not understand a word of the conversation, but Josh seemed unperturbed. She gave him credit for his patience.

When she had completed conversing with Quanah, Jael spoke to Josh. "Quanah says the People must leave this place soon. There are too many to feed. The game has been killed and eaten. There is no grazing for the surviving horses. The Comanche are nomads. They have always moved to other abundant places before they ravage and destroy the earth, as has been done here. But if they leave, the soldiers will kill them. Most of the warriors are too weak to fight."

"Ask him how soon his people will be ready to leave for the reservation."

She interpreted for Quanah, who gave an abrupt response. She spoke again to Josh. "Tomorrow, he says."

"Tell him I will ask Wolf to carry a message to Colonel Mackenzie that the Kwahadi are willing to go to the reservation on the terms I have discussed. I will ask the colonel to send an emissary who will confirm the agreement. In the meantime, he may commence preparing for departure."

Jael spoke again to the war chief, who was silent for several minutes. His face was a portrait of sadness when he replied at some length.

Jael interpreted. "Do this. The Kwahadi will embark on the dismal trail with hope that Bad Hand Mackenzie will keep his promises. Even so, on that day, freedom for the Comanche dies."

It was after sundown when Josh and Jael returned to the tipi. The others were finishing supper, a joint effort of Wolf, Tabitha, and Rylee. There was hot coffee, bacon, beans and biscuits. Jael noticed that Tabitha and Wolf were eating like they were starved, and then she realized they probably were. The supplies they had brought with them could provide a feast for a few, but not even scraps for a village of this size. Yet, she could not help but feel a little guilt about their momentary prosperity of foodstuffs. Servings had been saved for Jael and Josh, and she did not turn down her share.

As they ate, Josh explained the need to get a message to Mackenzie. "I must stay here to lay the groundwork for the peace conference," Josh said. "Oliver, I know you have work waiting in Santa Fe. Would you be able to deliver a message to Mackenzie at Fort Sill before you head to New Mexico?"

"Certainly, I was planning to check on the house renovation there, anyway. I have been thinking about it, and I recommend we cut out another entryway directly to the residential section. If you do not have an employee living there, you would probably not wish to have your tenant entering through the office area. We would still have the connecting doorway, but it could be locked if you chose."

"That makes sense. I'll leave that to you. I established a line of credit for the firm with the trading post before I left, and you're authorized to sign for materials. The carpenters understand I will issue bank drafts for their work when I return."

Tabitha interrupted. "Oliver told me about the project. I made some suggestions. I hope that was okay."

"It doesn't matter to me, as long as Oliver approves. I have no interest in the details. I just want it completed."

"When do you want me to leave?" Oliver asked.

"The sooner the better."

"Hey, don't forget me," Cal interjected. "I've got to get out of here. If Erin's back from visiting the Slash R, she's dreaming up tortures the Comanche couldn't think of."

"You're not fit to travel yet," Josh replied.

"Day after tomorrow. I'll be ready."

Josh looked at Jael. "What do you think?"

"I think he well have a painful journey, but it will not likely kill him. It may be suitable penance for his misbehavior. I remember Erin from the year she lived in our village, and I suspect she will add to his punishment." She smiled. "Of course, he will use the wound to his advantage, I am certain. I will send some of the poultice along, and Oliver can clean and treat his wound daily."

"I don't see any sympathy coming from here," Cal grumbled.

"Then you'll be leaving day after tomorrow?" Tabitha asked.

Jael thought she detected some distress in her friend's voice. Somehow, she did not think that the prospect of

Cal's leaving was bothering her. She wondered if something had happened between Wolf and Tabitha during her absence.

Wolf asked, "What do you want me to tell Colonel Mackenzie?"

"That Quanah has promised to come in and knows of the commitments the colonel has made. Ask him to send an emissary, who still should be instructed to make a persuasive case to Quanah and Isa-tai, who has somehow wormed his way back into a position of influence. Tell him that the Kwahadi are starving and ask him to order his troops to stand down and allow the Comanche to hunt during their journey to the reservation. Above all, inform him that time is of the essence because there are many Kwahadi who oppose Quanah's road to peace."

"I can do this."

42

"YOU SHOULD TAKE Michael on a hunt with you and teach him to use a rifle," Jael said.

"I don't know that I'm the best teacher. You're a better shot than I am, and Tabby's better than anybody."

"That is not the point. A boy should learn such things from his father."

"But Pop didn't allow us to handle a rifle until we were nine years old. Well, Tabby was an exception. Pop put a rifle in her hands at seven. Really upset the rest of us kids. She was a spoiled brat."

"And Michael will be seven years in the fall. And he is Comanche. It is time."

They stood in front of the tipi, a balmy breeze whisking their faces, and the early morning sun dropping rays of warmth on their backs. Josh did not know what the date was—he lost track when he was away from calendars—but he guessed they were in the early days of April.

"I guess we could do that."

"Michael has packed his things and will ride my mare. I chose one of the packhorses I brought with me from San Angelo, and, after a week's rest, I suspect Buck is ready for an outing."

"You think we should leave today?"

"Why not?"

"Well—" He could not think of a reason. "I guess we could go. I suppose you have some suggestions where." He could not resist a stab of sarcasm.

"I think you should go north. Stay in the canyon. Any Kwahadi renegades tend to stay south. If you encountered soldiers, they would not harm you."

"That makes sense. I guess it won't take me long to get a few things together. We don't have any food to pack."

"I have taught Michael about the roots and other vegetation in the wild that may be eaten, and, who knows, you may even shoot a rabbit."

She gave that single-dimple smile again. Somehow it charmed and annoyed him at the same time. He guessed it was because the smile usually showed up when she was needling him about something.

A few hours later, Josh and Michael were headed north into the south end of Palo Duro Canyon which extended northward for well over a hundred miles. They had decided to take two packhorses, Josh choosing to be an optimist about hunting prospects.

They rode along the creek that Josh thought was the Prairie Dog Town Fork of the Red River that snaked its way through the canyon floor. Josh had to admit Jael's idea had been a good one. He liked the feeling of being alone with his son away from Jael's ever-watchful eyes. She had made a sudden turn on the trek back from Fort Concho. Overnight, she had become a participant in establishing his connection with Michael, pushing the two males together whenever possible, seemingly laying a trail to ease the passage to bonding as father and son. The progress moved more slowly than he would have liked, but he knew Jael could have obstructed if she had chosen.

Life sharing the tipi with three females was not that comfortable and pleasant. Tabby had turned moody and irritable since Wolf's departure a week earlier. Rylee was a pleasant and energetic girl, but, whenever Michael was absent, all she wanted to talk about were schemes for making money when she and Jael went to Denver. Jael seemed to share her enthusiasm, but it irritated him that she had evidently discarded the notion of working for Rivers and Sinclair at Fort Sill. Furthermore, he did not desire to cut Michael off entirely from the woman he saw as his mother. He supposed, if he was to be honest with himself, he was resistant as well to being totally separated from Jael.

The firm badly needed her skills at Sill, Michael needed her accessibility, and, damn it, he would miss her presence in his life. This was getting too complicated.

They camped in the shelter of some spindly cottonwoods along the creek. Josh had made a lucky shot and killed a rabbit along the way, so they would have supper. He was pleased to find his son so adept with a skinning knife, as the skinning and disemboweling of a critter had never been his favorite chore. He quickly built a fire, and soon they were roasting chunks of rabbit impaled on green willow sticks.

Before he crawled into his buffalo robe, which was spread out next to Josh's bedroll, Michael asked, "When do you teach me to shoot the rifle?"

"First thing in the morning."

"I can load a Winchester."

"You can?"

"Mother taught me how to load hers . . . and Aunt Tabby's Henry, too."

"But she never let you shoot it?"

"No. She said I wasn't old enough. She did not learn until Aunt Tabby taught her. Aunt Tabby killed a soldier. Did you know that?"

"No." And he did not want to know any more about that or anything else his little sister might have done. "We'd better get some sleep. Busy day tomorrow."

"I am wondering about something."

"What is it?"

"What do I call you?"

Josh only realized at that moment the boy had evidently been carefully avoiding calling him anything. "Well, what do you want to call me? I call my father, 'Pop.' Some boys just say 'Father.' Others call their fathers 'Dad.'"

"I think I like 'Dad.'"

"Dad would be good. I would like that."

"Good night, Dad."

"Good night, Son."

43

ICHAEL TOOK TO the rifle instantly. The Winchester had a bit of a kick for a boy his size, and Josh saw him flinch a time or two after firing a shot but never heard a complaint. It occurred to him he had not heard the boy complain about anything during the time they had shared since San Angelo. He wondered if that was the result of Comanche culture or his mother's influence.

He finally had to declare a halt to the firing practice. Josh considered himself no better than average as a marksman, but he was confident his son would surpass his father's skills easily over the next few years. Maybe he could challenge for Tabby's family championship.

As they rode deeper into the canyon, Josh noted more evidence of game. They scared up several turkeys, and Josh fired a shot at one but missed. Michael suffered a similar fate with his shot at a rabbit. Michael pointed out raccoon prints and deer tracks along the muddy banks of the creek. Josh was not excited about eating coon, but he knew men who considered the animal a delicacy. Deer were more enticing. He had not taken down a doe since he and Cassie lived at the Slash R, several months before Michael was abducted and his wife and mother raped and murdered.

"Let's stake the horses and walk," Josh said. "We're making too much noise."

After staking the horses in a small meadow along the outer line of the trees, Josh and Michael quietly moved further upstream and then sought shelter in the trees and waited. Almost an hour later a young buck stepped cautiously out of the brush, stopping from time to time and sniffing the air suspiciously as he moved toward the river and a drink. They were hidden no more than thirty feet from the buck, and Josh signaled to Michael that he was going to fire first and then Michael should follow. Then he took careful aim and squeezed the trigger. The buck leaped and seemed stunned. Michael's rifle cracked, and the deer began to run.

Father and son jumped up and took off after the buck. A trail of blood indicated that one of them had made a hit. A quarter of a mile later, they found the dead victim stretched beneath a cottonwood tree. A quick examination showed two wounds, one neck, and the other above the shoulder, so each had sent a bullet home. That was fitting, Josh thought. Michael had already cut the buck's throat and was engaged with his skinning knife, so Josh removed his own, and together they butchered the deer. When they were about finished, Josh returned to retrieve the horses. Jael had sent salt she had purchased in San Angelo for preserving the meat, and they needed to salvage everything they could from this kill.

That evening Michael roasted slices of liver, a Comanche delicacy, while Josh settled for flank steak. They ate till they were stuffed. When he had finished eating, Michael asked, "Dad, what are you going to do about the one who follows?"

"What do you mean? Someone is following us?"

"I thought you knew. He has been following us since morning. The birds became quiet behind us, and, once, I looked back and saw the shadow of a horse and rider on the canyon wall. I am sure there is only one."

"Well, we had better find out what he has in mind."

"I can find him."

"No, it is too dangerous."

"I will not get near him. I will only see who he is and where he is at."

How could he argue with the boy? Boots were not made for stealth, and Josh had no demonstrable skills at tracking and stalking. Such things were innate to Michael's upbringing. "Okay. But don't get too close."

Michael leaped up and disappeared like a slinky cat into the trees. Josh waited by the fire, feeding the low flames just enough wood to keep the embers hot. It seemed like the wait carried on for hours, but his pocket watch said only forty-five minutes had elapsed when Michael startled him by his sudden appearance at his side. He would have to tie a bell on this kid.

"It is Growling Bear," Michael said.

"Should I know him?"

"Quanah sends him and Scratching Turkey with Mother when she goes to talk to people. He means us no harm."

"I remember him. A big man?"

"Yes, but he has been hungry like others of the People. Now he is not so big. More like his spirit animal after a winter's sleep."

"I wonder what he is doing here?"

"I think Mother sent him to watch over us."

Josh felt his anger surge, and he fought to control his words in the presence of his young son. It would serve no purpose criticize the boy's mother. He would save his words for her. "Wouldn't it be easier for him to watch over us if he was with us?"

"What do you mean?"

"He may be hungry. Do you want to invite him over to eat?"

The boy grinned. "That would be fun. He thinks we are easily fooled."

"One of us is. Why don't you go call him in for supper?"

Again, Michael vanished. But this time he was gone less than a half hour before he reappeared with Growling Bear, who had a very sheepish look on his face. Josh raised a hand in greeting. "Tell him to slice whatever he wants of the venison and to roast it on our fire while we counsel."

Michael spoke rapidly in Comanche, and the warrior, who appeared gaunt and weary, replied and went to the cuts of meat strung out on braided rawhide ropes on the tree branches. He took out his knife and helped himself to a slice of liver, one of the testicles and an assortment of other cuts. Using the crude utensils Michael and Josh had cut earlier, he began roasting the meat over the fire. The poor man was starving, Josh thought, as he watched Growling Bear roast and eat the venison.

"He thanks us for our generosity," Michael said. "His hunting was not so good today."

"Ask Growling Bear if your mother sent him."

The warrior seemed reluctant to reply at first, but then he evidently thought better of it and responded.

Michael said, "He says my mother asked him to follow us. We were not to know unless we found trouble. He worries that my mother will be displeased."

"Tell him to ride with us. That way he will be nearby if we need his help."

After Michael extended the invitation, the warrior seemed relieved. After he had finished eating, he left to retrieve his ponies.

Josh figured after another day and night they should return to the village. He hoped they might bring down another deer to provide more meat for the village.

The next day his hopes became reality. Michael shot a doe for an undisputed kill, and with his bow and arrows, Growling Bear took down a doe and old buck. Josh harvested another young buck. They agreed that Michael's mare would be pressed into packhorse duties, and that the boy would ride behind Josh on Buck for the return trip. That would enable the party to carry all the carcasses back to the village.

As they prepared to head south and locate a campsite for the night, they heard what Josh thought sounded like a cow bawling for a lost calf. Growling Bear said something to Michael, who translated. "He says that was a buffalo, and where there is one there are more. He wants us to leave the horses here and follow the water north upstream."

"Tell him we will follow but must return here before dark."

Growling Bear led the way and in less than half hour they came to the edge of a meadow carved out in the middle of all the brush and small trees. Before them were a grazing herd of bison, shaggy and somewhat mottled from the winter coats they were starting to shed. The grass was new growth here, fresh and green, and the sun was starting to bid farewell as it crept over the top of the canyon wall. The evening was calm and warm. Josh thought they were viewing what an artist might characterize as a pastoral scene.

Growling Bear seemed not to be captured by the aesthetics of the view. He appeared all business and looked like he was making a tally. Soon he spoke excitedly.

Michael said, "He counts nearly two hundred buffalo. Not a big herd but not small for these times. We must tell Quanah now. A good hunt could save the lives of many of the People."

44

WOLF WAS ANXIOUS to return to Santa Fe, hoping he could sweep the nagging memories of Tabitha Rivers from his mind there. He took some consolation from Tabitha's light kiss on his cheek and warm hug before he saddled up and rode off with Cal Rivers. She would see him in Santa Fe, she had promised. Perhaps their story was not over, but it was time for him to get on with his life.

Cal had left Fort Sill this morning, settling for a two-day layover prior to the journey to the McKenna Ranch and a rendezvous with his wife, Erin. Wolf suspected that Cal was not so fearful of the reunion as he professed. It was impossible to dislike the man, even though he was something of a rogue, and he suspected Cal would literally charm the woman out of her underthings upon his arrival home. The former scout had recovered nicely from his wound during their ten-day trip. He had been appreciative of Wolf's nightly dressing of the wound, and they had formed a solid friendship during that time. Strangely, Cal had not complained once, and Wolf suspected the man tailored his dialogue to his audience, realizing sympathy from his companion would not be forthcoming. Wolf smiled as he speculated about what stories Erin would hear from her husband about his latest adventures. Cal was a man who did not let truth get in the way of a good tale, especially if it was a self-serving one.

Wolf was sitting in the outer office of the post commander's headquarters now, waiting for his audience with Colonel Mackenzie. He had reported here promptly upon arrival the day previous, but the young corporal at the desk had seemed disinterested in Wolf's desire to meet with the new post commander, and Wolf had left. Wolf generally shrugged off paranoia about prejudice, but he wondered if a white man would not have received more attention. In any event, the same corporal had been assigned yesterday to track him down and advise him of his appointment this morning and to assure him that the commanding officer looked forward to meeting with him. The corporal was not on duty this morning, and Wolf suspected the young man had lost his desk job.

The middle-aged sergeant at the desk this morning had tendered a cup of coffee for Wolf to enjoy while he waited, and they had exchanged a few pleasantries. The brew was a welcome change from the mud Cal concocted when they were on the trail to Sill. Mackenzie's office door opened, and a flinty-looking, white-haired major came out. He nodded at Wolf as he passed by. Shortly, Colonel Ranald Slidell Mackenzie followed.

The slouched, rumpled Mackenzie appeared much less the commanding officer than the man, probably ten years his senior, who had preceded him. He extended his good hand to Wolf as the Cherokee rose from his chair. "White Wolf. Good to see you again. I am informed you have important news. Come in and tell me about it."

Mackenzie led Wolf into a small, austere office with a single window that looked out onto the parade grounds. When they were both seated, Mackenzie said, "I trust you have some word from Josh Rivers."

"I do, General," Wolf said, intentionally addressing Mackenzie by his brevet rank. "Josh believes Quanah is ready to come to the reservation. He says it is urgent that you send emissaries to put arrangements in place." He then described the current plight of the Kwahadi and affirmed his own belief that the time was right for peace.

Mackenzie said, "Mr. Rivers continues to emphasize his terms. I explained to him at our earlier meeting that Quanah has no leverage for dictating terms."

"Perhaps not, but Josh Rivers received certain assurances and believes your word is good. He is also convinced, as I am, that Quanah is a man of enormous political skills and that the two of you can forge an alliance that will be very productive to your command and promote his rise in influence among the chiefs."

"You appear to have your own political skills, Mr. Wolf. I assure you that I will do everything within my power to keep the commitments I made to Mr. Rivers. Election politics may keep the bureaucrats and politicians out of our way if we proceed and accomplish this quietly and without fanfare. President Grant and much of Congress are absorbed in their political campaigns this year. If we can get Quanah to come in without any more bloodshed, I think I can make our welcome here more congenial to him."

"I am pleased to hear those words, General."

"I am going to send Dr. Sturm as translator and negotiator, along with Chief Wild Horse and a few other Comanche as emissaries. I will see if they can leave within the week. Could you meet with Dr. Sturm and Wild Horse and tell them how to find Quanah, perhaps share any insights you have as to how the delegation should approach the so-called peace negotiations?"

"I would be pleased to do this, sir. It so happens I am lodging at Dr. Sturm's hospital. I will see him as soon as I leave here and arrange a meeting with him and Wild Horse."

After leaving Mackenzie's office, Wolf went directly to inform Sturm he would be receiving a message soon from the commanding officer about leading a peace delegation to Quanah's village. Sturm, being a civilian, was not subject to military orders, but he seemed always on the lookout for a way to make a dollar—and had no objection if a little prestige or fame was incident to his work. Sturm agreed to locate Wild Horse to work out a meeting for the next morning. That task completed, Wolf returned to the Rivers and Sinclair project, where he had spent most of the previous day.

Wolf was pleased with the craftsmanship of the Army carpenters, several of whom had been able to work on the office-residence quite regularly during his absence. He speculated that, drawn by the carrot of private pay, the soldiers might have been neglecting some Army duties, but he asked no questions. Sergeant Walter Shales, an exceptionally skilled cabinet maker, had taken a special interest in the stone house, and Wolf thought the noncom might have had some influence in diverting some of the Army's construction talent to the project.

Wolf had personally chiseled out the limestone to form the opening for the doorway he had not included in the original plans. Wally Shales assured him he would personally build and install a fine door. The sagging roof had been replaced, so spring rains were no longer a threat to the interior. He felt comfortable leaving the project under the supervision of the sergeant, but Tabitha, upon being told about the renovation, had suggested he should acquire some basic furnishings for the place. She said Josh would have no interest in this and likely would not think about it till he realized he had no chair to sit in or a desk to work at. Caught up in the planning herself now, she had even compiled a list of furniture and household items she felt were needed. He scratched his head over some of her demands, which seemed excessive.

The post commissary filled the order for Dutch ovens, pots, pans and other basics and even turned up a serviceable cook and heating stove. The furniture had all been commandeered by one officer or another, so Wolf rode out to a saw mill that had started up a business a few miles from the post and found an assortment of oak and other native hardwoods and had them delivered to the house. He figured he could stay on a few more weeks, and he and Wally would build enough furniture for the occupants to get by. Wally had been excited at the prospect of building furniture, but Wolf warned him there would be nothing ornate. Simple and sturdy would be their objective. He had to admit, though, he was enthusiastic about returning to work that his mind could create and implement via his skilled hands. It might help him to direct his thoughts away from Tabitha.

45

THERE WAS REBELLION to put down in the tipi. Michael claimed he should be entitled to go on the buffalo hunt because he had been with the finders of the herd and he had killed a deer with a rifle. Jael told him he was too young and that a deer was not a buffalo. Rylee wanted to kill a buffalo, and Tabitha wanted to write about the hunt. Jael pointed out that someone must stay with Michael and that the sick and infirm in the village could not be abandoned. The stronger women and men would be needed to either kill or butcher the buffalo and haul meat and hides back. Tabitha and Rylee would do more good in the village, she insisted. Tabitha countered that she could outshoot anyone in the village and that she had butchered countless deer and a good number of cattle in her lifetime. Josh said nothing, he just lay back against his bedroll, hands clasped behind his head, and smiled as if he was enjoying the turmoil. He was really irking her.

Finally, Jael capitulated. "Okay, we will all go on the hunt. Even Josh. We can surely find some task he is capable of helping with." She tried to give him her fiercest look, but his annoying smile did not change.

Several days later the Kwahadi hunting party set up camp not far from where Josh said they had heard the bellow of the buffalo cow. Scouts confirmed that the herd still grazed the meadow. The band had gathered up nearly thirty warriors for the hunt and might have had twice as many, but small hunting parties wandered throughout the plains seeking game, and many had not heard of the find. There were at least forty women, young and old, and some children who would butcher the kills.

Quanah had joined the hunting party, but he deferred to a warrior who was a renowned hunter and, for all practical purposes, the hunt chief. Regardless of his ambitions, Quanah was still considered a war chief, and it would be impolitic for him to overreach his authority. It was not acceptable for a woman to ride with the warriors who attacked the herd, but recognizing her prowess with a bow, the war chief instructed Jael to take Josh and Tabitha around the grazing herd to try to act as barriers if any of the animals stampeded north. They were to take buffalo robes to wave and try to turn back the frantic beasts and to kill any that they were able. Jael recognized this as an important and dangerous, but unsung, job. She doubted and worried that Josh and Tabitha did not.

Rylee and Michael, now Flying Crow again for this day, were assigned by the hunt chief to help the women with the skinning and butchering. They accepted their assignments without protest since Jael had not issued the order.

The morning of the hunt, since Josh knew the location of the herd, Jael asked him to lead their party past the animals to their appointed stations. Leading Buck, Josh swung away from the river until he reached a canyon wall and began to follow it northward. They made an unusual caravan for a buffalo hunt, led by a white man, followed by two women, one in buckskin britches and her late husband's war shirt and the other dressed like a working cowboy. Behind them came a tall, lanky girl in canvas trousers and striped wool shirt and a boy in a breechclout and doeskin vest and two younger, bony Comanche women. Interspersed were mounts and a collection of packhorses to help carry the salvaged skins and meat. They were too many, Jael thought, and she was glad Josh had chosen to make a wide swath to by-pass the herd. They dared not spook the buffalo; many lives depended upon their success this day.

When they had passed by the herd, Josh turned back toward the creek. The herd was not likely within hearing distance, but Jael spoke softly, first in English and then Comanche. "We cannot protect the entire canyon floor. It is many miles wide. Our warriors will try to drive the beasts away from the other side by focusing the attack from there. We are at the end of a funnel, so to speak. The hunters hope to make many kills before the buffalo reach here, but we are to try to turn them back, and if we cannot, kill as many as we can. Be prepared to wave blankets and robes if you see a buffalo, but do not be foolish . . . run to safety if it does not stop. Josh and Tabitha, you may ride your horses while you try to turn the animals, but you will probably want to dismount and seek cover if they become too many."

They spread out over as much of the area as feasible, but Jael could see that the best strategy was to kill as many of the buffalo as possible, building a barricade of bodies. She had as many as twenty arrows in her quiver. She had told Joshua and Tabitha to aim for a spot between the neck and front shoulder of the buffalo. Tabitha had her Henry, and Josh a Winchester, but she did not know how effective these guns were against a mighty buffalo. She had been told about the powerful rifles of the white buffalo hunters that would kill at great distances, but her own experience with the smaller rifles made her dubious. The bullets might prove to be mere gnats nipping at a buffalo hide. Perhaps at closer range they would be useful.

Suddenly, she heard the thunder of hooves and the whoops of her Comanche brothers in the distance. The killing had started. Her eyes searched for Michael and Rylee. As instructed, Rylee was no more than a dozen feet from Jael's son. She was confident the girl would drag Michael into the nearby woods, if necessary, when she sensed danger. Sometimes one had to trust another. And she trusted Rylee.

She guessed an hour passed before the first buffalo emerged from the brush and saplings that cloaked so much of the canyon floor. It was a cow with calf at her side. She saw Josh and Tabitha gig their horses toward the cow, waving their robes rapidly. The wild-eyed cow would have nothing of it; she lunged forward. Jael nocked an arrow and nudged her mare closer, gripping the horse tightly with her knees. She let an arrow loose, and it struck true, plunging into the cow's lower neck above the shoulder. The cow took only a few steps before her front legs buckled, and she stumbled forward and crashed to the ground. Jael saw Tabitha raise her rifle and aim at the calf that nosed its dying mother. The gun cracked, and the calf dropped. Good. That saved an arrow, and the calf would have died without its mother.

Soon, another cow appeared, and then a half-grown bull. She took the cow down with two arrows, and Josh shot the bull. Perhaps he was a bit self-deprecating about his marksmanship. Tabitha dropped another cow, and after that the remnants of the herd came on faster, and she stopped her count. She was rapidly depleting her supply of arrows, and she had too many misses from horseback, so she dismounted to gain steadier footing from which to release her missiles. The mare raced away, but she would not go far. It was a melee now, but the animals were dispersed.

Jael launched an arrow that hit a cow in the shoulder but did not bring her down. As she reached over her shoulder to pluck another arrow from the quiver, she heard the distinctive roar of an angry bull behind her and whirled to see a massive head with horns lowered and charging not more than twenty-five feet away. She froze for just an instant, and then the muscular body of Joshua's buckskin gelding blocked her line of vision. She saw Josh's arm reach out, but before she could grab his hand, the horse shrieked and tumbled over, pinning the rider underneath. She saw that the bull had driven his horns into the gelding's side, and when the beast pulled back for just an instant, readying to renew his charge, part of the victim's intestines clung to his horns.

Josh was anchored to the ground by the flailing horse, and the bull would be on him in a moment. Knowing she would be too late, she stepped back and nocked her arrow with shaky fingers. Abruptly, the horse fought to rise again and took another blow from the enraged bull, but not before allowing Joshua to roll free. This time, she was ready and drove an arrow into the monster's neck. And then another. And another. The bull kept coming and staggered over the buckskin before collapsing, his massive head dropping just inches from Josh's own. A wave of relief had swept over her when she saw Josh pull his leg out from underneath the dying horse and slowly pick himself up. Her euphoria evaporated now as she watched a grim-faced man retrieve the Winchester he had dropped when he tumbled with the horse.

Tears rolled down her cheeks when the man placed the rifle barrel to the head of his old friend and squeezed the trigger.

46

JAEL DID NOT know what to say to Josh after the attack by the bull buffalo. His intervention clearly saved her life, and he narrowly escaped with his own. Buck's timely last effort had salvaged just enough time for her to nock and loose her arrows.

He had not given her an opportunity to thank him. After quickly relieving the gelding of its suffering, Josh had knelt beside the dead horse and gently stroked its head and muzzle, apparently saying his last good-bye. He then removed the horse's saddle and bridle, with his coiled rope and other tack, and silently carried it away without so much as a glance in her direction.

Somehow, the incident signaled the hunt was ended, and the Comanche women descended on the carnage with skinning knives and deerskin bags. Soon they were all absorbed in the bloody, back-breaking work of eviscerating, skinning and butchering eleven dead buffalo scattered in the dry grass and dirt about them. Jael noticed that two women were sharing slices of a liver as they worked, and Michael had accepted an offer of a small chunk and downed it quickly. Rylee had politely declined a taste, but not surprisingly, she learned the tasks quickly and, after a few hours apprenticeship, recruited Michael to help her process one of the calves. Mid-afternoon Quanah and Growling Bear showed up to inspect the harvest. The war chief nodded approvingly. "A good last hunt," he said. "She Who Speaks has done well." She had not thought of it that way. The buffalo hunt was more than a necessity for sustaining Comanche life. It was a huge social event, almost spiritual in its importance. And this was probably the last hunt for the Kwahadi, symbolic for the end of their way of life.

Quanah said that the kills totaled forty-five and promised to send help to finish the butchering and packing of the meat. He was anxious to return with a feast for his starving village, and she could see that he was not likely to be unduly modest about his role in the hunt.

She had just started to skin and butcher the big bull when Josh knelt beside her with his skinning knife and began the slices to peel the tough hide. She had been mildly surprised to find he was not a novice at the processing of an animal, but she supposed a boy growing up on a mountain ranch would have naturally learned such things. Two working on the huge carcass sped up the process. She found they worked together well, and although they exchanged no more than a few words, each anticipated the other's cuts, and they dressed the animal efficiently.

When they were finished, she stood up and surveyed the killing site. Their work was about complete. Others had arrived to help pack the meat. She and Joshua were blood-soaked, but so was everyone else. A bath in the clear creek would be welcome. It was spring-fed and would be ice-cold, but she promised herself this treat later.

Josh spoke from behind her. "I'm going to bury Buck."

She turned and looked at him incredulously. Nobody buried horses. "You are going to bury him? Where? How?"

"There's a little sandstone butte about fifty yards further north. Mostly sand and dirt on the walls. I'll borrow Tabby's horse and drag him up there. I can cave-in part of the butte over him. And stack some loose stones on top. I don't want him being buzzard and coyote food."

"You may use my horse. I will help."

He shrugged.

Jael told Tabitha of their plans to bury Buck. "It is strange, but Josh and Buck saved my life, and I feel I must help."

"It's not so strange when you know Josh. He's hard to get next to. He's what some call a loner. He's always got close to his critters, a horse, or a dog, even a cat. Oh, he's got lots of acquaintances and gets along with folks, but nobody really knows him. I'm probably his closest sib, but he keeps me guessing about what's really going on in that head of his. Anyway, Pop gave Buck to Josh when he was just a foal, and they were best friends for a dozen or more years."

"Well, I will try to be useful with the burial. I assure you my Comanche tribesmen would find this very humorous, even though they have great affection for horses."

"You stay here with Josh. I will leave Michael's horse for Josh, and Michael can ride double with me or Rylee. We will ride back with the others and take the packhorses and hides and meat with us."

"You could stay here, and we could all go back together tomorrow."

"Yes, I certainly could, but I will not." Tabitha called for Rylee and Michael and told them to start gathering up their things and to unsaddle Michael's horse.

Jael retrieved her mare, which, as she was confident would be the case, had not wandered far. Josh had already hitched his rope to Buck's hind legs by the time she led the skittish mare up to the dead horse. He anchored the other end of the rope by looping it around the mare's chest and then tying it to the saddle horn, making a crude harness.

"Do you think she can pull the load?" she asked.

"It's mostly flat and then down a gentle slope at the end, and I'll help pull. You'll need to lead and encourage her."

It was a slow journey, but Josh was right about the sloping terrain over the last part of the route. The mare was tired-out by the time they maneuvered Buck into position by the butte, and, as Jael led her away to stake out in the grass with Michael's gelding, Jael figured the sorrel would be less contrary about saddle horse duties in the future.

They had no shovels, but Jael found a flat piece of limestone the size of a big shovel blade that she made serviceable, and Josh chopped a rotting slab of cottonwood into a scooping tool, and they both clambered to the top of the butte, which was no more than a dozen feet high, and got down on hands and knees and began digging and caving away dirt and sand to cover the buckskin gelding. They worked in near silence for the better part of two hours, and it was nearly sunset before the horse was covered to Joshua's satisfaction.

"I'll see if I can find some rocks to layer the top with in the morning," he said. "Right now, I'll start a fire, and we can enjoy a few of the buffalo steaks we carved out today."

"I would like to go to the creek and bathe and change, if you don't mind. I will not take long."

"Go right ahead. I'll do the same after we eat."

As she had anticipated, she nearly froze in the creek, but it was worth every goose bump to feel clean again. She didn't have any more doeskins in her saddlebags, so she dug out the baggy canvas britches and red wool shirt she had purchased in Santa Fe. She found a pair of cotton underpants, and that was more underneath than she was accustomed to. She thought she might try to wash her filthy and bloodied garments in the morning.

Jael followed the sweet smell of the smoke to the fire until she saw the dancing flames. She hurried to the promise of warmth because it was still cool at night this time of year, and she had not yet recovered from her bath. She was surprised to find strips of roasted buffalo meats laid out on a flat stone next to the fire. Her canteen was there, and her buffalo sleeping robe was spread out, too, layered with an extra blanket. It had been placed a dozen feet from Josh's own, much like its location in the tipi her peculiar family shared. Family. Strange way to think of their little group.

"Dinner is served," Josh said, as he stood up in front of the fire. "You'll have to pardon my manners, though. I went ahead and ate, and now I'm going to try my luck with the bath. I hope it's warmer than I think it is."

"It is not. But you still won't be sorry."

He picked up his saddlebags. "I need a shave . . . it's been four days . . . but my little camp mirror shattered when Buck came down on my saddlebags."

"Do you have a straight-edge and soap?"

"Yes. Why?"

"I can shave you. I used to shave my father sometimes. I shaved him the morning . . . never mind."

"It would take some trust for me to let you put a straight-edge next to my throat."

"Yes, I suppose it would."

"I'll think on it."

47

THE LADY WAS a pretty fair barber, Josh had to admit. She had been forced to work in the firelight and resting on her knees, and there was nary a nick. She had used part of his sole bandana to wash the soap off and the remainder of it to dry, and it felt darn good. The loss of Buck still weighed heavily on him, but the shave had revitalized him, and it had been fun as they had bantered back and forth about her control of the blade.

He sat on his robe now, staring skyward at nothing special because his mind was not following his eyes. Jael sat on her robe, too, and Josh was struck by the silliness of the physical distance between them. But he had set things up that way, so he had no one else to blame. As if hearing his unspoken thought, Jael stood up and drug her robe and blanket over and laid it out next to his. She sat down, only a few feet from him now.

"Don't you feel it's foolish for us to have to carry on this long-distance conversation when there are just the two of us?" she asked. "Besides, if I were going to harm you, I missed my chance."

"I welcome your company."

"I haven't thanked you for saving my life. So, thank you."

"He would have killed me if you hadn't been there with your bow, so I'd say we're even on that score."

"Why did you take the risk?"

"It never occurred to me to do otherwise. It's all instinct and reaction at times like that. I've thought about it a lot since. I'll never totally get over Buck's death, and I'll never forget this day. In a way, intentional or not, he gave us both the rest of our lives. It could have ended for both of us in an instant. Each day's a bonus now and we'd do darn well to think seriously about what we're going to do with each bonus."

"I've thought that ever since my parents were killed and I was taken by the Comanche. Why was I not killed, too? That loss and my life before, strangely, is only starting to come back to me. But I realized soon after that day I had been spared, and I had better make the most of it."

"When it was over, do you know what horrified me most?"

"I can't imagine."

"How terrible it would have been for Michael to see his mother die like that. And what an injustice it would have been for him to lose two loving and wonderful mothers in a span of half a dozen years."

"But it would have been a tragedy for him to lose his father as well."

"Not as much so. I think he is coming to like me well enough, but I haven't earned the title yet. I hope to someday. I've been given the opportunity."

She reached over and placed her hand over his, and, casual and natural as her action was, it sent a jolt through his body. "Joshua, I want you to understand something. I trust you to care for Michael. It will not be easy for me to give him up, but I have come to terms with this, in my mind, if not within my heart. I have come to see the kind of man you are, and I have no fear for my son's future. I love him enough to let him go."

He turned to her and placed a hand gently on her cheek, and spoke softly. "I kissed you once, and you pulled away. What if I kissed you now?"

"I would not pull away."

He leaned toward Jael and pressed his lips to hers, first softly, and then hungrily, and she moved to him, holding him tight, like she feared he might get up and run away. And then they were naked, lying on one of their robes, and he could not recall how that came to be. He only knew they felt right together, and he succumbed easily to her willingness to join him on a journey that was only theirs to share.

He woke in the middle of the night and knew he had not been dreaming when he felt her warm body spooned against his back and her arm wrapped snuggly about his waist. He wanted her again but hesitated to awaken her.

"Yes," she said drowsily. "I think we should."

48

THE PEOPLE ATE again for several weeks before the supply of buffalo meat dwindled. Josh was anxious to start the journey to the reservation. They could not replenish food supplies staying at this place. If the soldiers did not interfere as they moved north, he guessed the Kwahadi would be able to range to hunt game. Where in the hell was Sturm? Has Mackenzie changed his mind? Josh's greatest fear was that some idiot in Washington would demand military victory and that many companies of cavalry would appear instead of the emissaries for peace.

One day, Jael reassured him. "Quanah says they will be here in five sunrises. He has warriors watching. Be patient."

She contributed to his restlessness. After the night they spent together, they rejoined the hunting party and returned to the village. Since that time, Jael acted as if nothing had ever happened between them. Of course, opportunities for intimacies were limited, just short of nonexistent. The five of them still shared a tipi. Comanche seemed not to suffer such inhibitions, but he was not about to crawl under Jael's robe with Tabitha, Rylee and Michael just a few feet away. He doubted Jael would welcome any such attempt, anyway.

Jael and Josh met daily with Quanah to discuss the coming move to the reservation. The sessions were redundant, the topics always the same, the questions unanswerable. Quanah had taken to practicing his English at these meetings, and Josh was surprised at his proficiency. He knew that Jael had continued to work with him on honing his language skills. Josh concluded the shrewd war chief would understand and speak English at his convenience. There were no doubt times when it was strategic to be thought of as an ignorant savage.

Isa-tai had been invited to some of their sessions lately. It was clear that Quanah had contempt for the medicine man and that he saw him as a rival. Sometimes one was well-advised to keep his enemies close. After one of the meetings, Jael explained that Isa-tai wanted to be the spokesman for the band at the peace conference. "Quanah always says 'we will see, we will see.' Yes, Quanah will see that he has no role that would leave Quanah in the shadows. Quanah is your client, so I assume you will suggest to the emissaries that Quanah is the true spokesman for the band."

"You can be devious, can't you?" Josh asked.

She responded only with a twinkle in her eyes and her single-dimpled smile.

One morning there was a commotion at the north end of the village, and Josh and Jael joined the other villagers who were rushing to see what was happening. They found a small party was slowly approaching the village with dozens of Comanche trailing behind. Josh immediately recognized Dr. Sturm, wearing a three-piece suit, at the head of the group. As the group approached, it appeared that the four others were Comanche. Josh and Jael strolled out to greet Sturm, who dismounted, and walked forward with his hand outstretched. After they shook hands, Sturm introduced his companions, the most notable of whom was Wild Horse. Two others were reservation Kwahadi, and the other represented a different band. All would tell the Kwahadi chiefs of the joys of life on the reservation.

Jael pointed out three tipis that had been set up on the edge of the village, two for lodging the guests and another very large one for accommodating the conferences. She informed the visitors that Quanah would appear soon to welcome them.

Sturm confided to Josh and Jael. "I am glad this is the last of them. I would never travel in this godforsaken country again. Hot, dry, dusty. I don't know why I'm here. I'm called an interpreter, but I can't hold a candle to this young lady in proficiency when it comes to Comanche dialects. I was unable to understand half of what my traveling companions were talking about. I hope, Miss Chernik, you will be attending these meetings."

"If that is your wish, sir. I am sure Quanah will include me."

The meetings continued for nearly two days, some sessions including as many as twenty of the tribal chiefs and elders and others limited to Quanah and Isa-tai. Josh attended those meetings and found himself becoming impatient again. The same speeches were given several times daily. The reservation Comanche emissaries spoke of endless beef and food supplies distributed to the Comanche and Kiowa residing there and the good times to be had by socializing with old friends and freed from the struggle for survival.

Isa-tai spoke many times of the affection he had come to have for the white people, claiming that as a medicine man he loved everyone and had the respect of the People.

He said that he had never harmed a white man, woman or child, notably omitting that his prophecies of invincibility had led to many battles, including the Comanche failure at Adobe Walls.

Quanah listened politely, but at the end of the first day he remarked to Jael, who interpreted for Josh, "They take me for a fool, thinking I would believe these stories. And even if they are true, what kind of man chooses not to provide for himself? If the Great White Father in Washington can give us these things, he can also take them away. We are forced to surrender, but if we are to regain any of our freedom, we must find other ways to escape this false benevolence."

Josh observed that Quanah seemed to respect Dr. Sturm, possibly because the interpreter-emissary was cautious with the promises he made. Also, Sturm held several lengthy private meetings with Quanah, which Jael speculated were arranged at Quanah's request to circumvent Isa-tai's grab for power. Quanah was determined to be the link between the white authorities and the Comanche, and to that end he informed Jael he wished to intensify his English studies on the trail to the reservation.participants all knew, the peace negotiations were a charade. Near the end of the second day, Quanah announced that the Kwahadi would depart for the reservation after the rising of four suns.

49

JAEL AND TABITHA knelt on the tipi floor sorting through the skins, pottery bowls, kettles and clothing, deciding what to discard and how much they could carry with them on the journey to the reservation. Jael had sent Josh, Rylee and Michael to build travois and stretchers for hauling the possessions that were not left behind. She was not in a mood for conversation, and none of the exiles would have been helpful in accomplishing this unpleasant task.

Tabitha said, "I had no idea we had this much stuff in here. I guess it was right in front of us, but I swear I never saw most of it. How much do we have to get rid of?"

"Probably three-fourths."

"What do we do with the surplus?"

"Leave it here. I will pass word that if anyone wants the tipi or anything left in it, they may take it. That is one reason I did not want Rylee here. She would want to take everything and try to sell it to somebody."

"You are abandoning the tipi?"

"What would we do with it? We would not want to put it up and take it down every stop on the journey. When we arrive at Fort Sill, we will have no need for it. None of us will remain on the reservation. I suppose you and Joshua and Michael will leave for Santa Fe as soon as possible. Rylee and I will seek passage to Denver."

"You're not serious? You're not going to take the law firm position near the reservation? What about you and Josh?"

"What about us?"

"Well, that night you stayed with him after the buffalo hunt. I guess I had hopes that something would happen between you."

"You were trying to make a match, weren't you? When you left us there?"

"Well—"

"I come from a Jewish family. I remembered recently that my mother told me about families employing matchmakers."

"Something happened between you and Josh. I know it did. Did you sleep with him?"

"I slept, yes. Quite well, thank you."

"That isn't what I meant, and you know it. Were you intimate with him?"

"Why would you even think that?"

"Because you are evading my question."

"Am I being interviewed for a newspaper story?"

"No, of course not. But for about eight months I've lived all this tragedy and sadness. My newspaper stories and my book will reflect this. But I desperately want to write a story with a happy ending, something uplifting that just makes the reader feel good. Perhaps you and Josh could inspire a novel I would write. Yes, a great love story that unfolds during the last days of the Comanche."

"Sometimes you show symptoms of lunacy. Write fairy tales if you seek happy endings." Jael knew her friend meant well. They were both young women in their early twenties, who had not seen all that much of life. But survival and brief intervals of joy were the most Jael hoped for, and neither could be taken for granted. Falling in love with Josh had been one of those intervals, and she would rather endure the pain of loss than never to have experienced it. She was confident he was a man she could spend a lifetime with, but how could he trust her? Her pursuit of him would seem so self-serving—selling herself to keep her son. She had been blindsided. She had not expected to fall in love with the father of her son. Now she must let go of both.

They moved the items they were taking with them outside the tipi. They stacked the buffalo robes and blankets and laid the rifles and ammunition and Jael's bow and quiver on top. The saddles and tack were placed together, and pots and other items that might be useful on the trail were all categorized and separated. Jael was by habit an organizer, and she did not intend to haul anything that would not have a purpose. She and Tabitha had selected the items of clothing they wished to take. Tabitha had arrived with nothing, so she would be leaving with a bit more. Jael decided to take only her deerskin shirts and britches, as well as the store-bought riding trousers and shirts. She would leave the dresses and other city garb behind. She had money and would buy more when she settled in Denver. The other tipi occupants would make their selections upon their return. It was a warm day, and the pale blue of the sky was unbroken by a single cloud. They would sleep under the stars tonight.

Josh and his two workers returned, dragging an assortment of trimmed poles and shorter pieces of cedar. She smiled at the animation and camaraderie among them. They had been working hard, but the shared mission bonded them, and that was always fun to watch, and, sometimes, be a part of. They dropped their harvest in front of the tipi.

"We have another load to fetch," Josh said, "but there is something we are curious about."

"Tell me," Jael said.

"There are fifteen to twenty old people, more men than women, gathered at the edge of the village. Nobody seems to be paying attention, but they look like they're gathering to leave the village. They don't have any horses, though. No food. A single buffalo robe for each."

"Take me to them."

Josh led her and Tabitha, with the two youngsters, to the assembly of ancients. When they arrived, she saw they were mostly Kwahadi, and there were twice as many men as women, over twenty in total now. The men were bent and frail. Several could barely stand or walked on trembling legs. The women had seen many years but seemed less decrepit for the most part. "Wait here," Jael said, as she separated from her tipi family and walked into the crowd of somber Indians. She saw a thin, bird-like woman, standing erect and proud next to an old man who sat on the ground, dozing with his head sagging against his chest. Calm Lark had befriended her from the day Jael arrived in the Kwahadi village those many years back. Kind and comforting with a soothing aura that put one immediately at ease with her, Calm Lark had been Jael's only confidante during her years with the Comanche. The woman would be close to eighty years of age now, and her face was tracked with deep, crisscrossed wrinkles that evidenced her years. But her body seemed strong after surviving the weeks of near starvation, and Jael knew her mind was clear and keen.

She approached the woman and embraced her gently. Then, speaking Comanche, they engaged in conversation for some time until they were interrupted by movement of the small mass of the People. Calm Lark bent and awakened the man who slept and leaned against her leg now. A warrior Jael recognized as Calm Lark's nephew— she had no children—led a mare, who was well past her prime of service, toward them, and Jael and the nephew helped the crippled old warrior onto the horse. Calm Lark took the reins, and, after briefly touching her nephew's cheek and giving Jael a reassuring smile, turned and led the mounted horse away, joining the shuffling march from the village that had already commenced.

When she rejoined the others, Tabitha, with her reporter's eye, had obviously recognized a story and was the first to speak. "What was that all about? Where are those people going?"

"They are taking the trail to meet the Great Spirit. They have chosen to die free. They will walk out onto the prairie until they can go no longer. Then they will wait to die. Some may be unable to travel as far others, so they will stop and wait for their time. Some may choose to stay with them. Others will go on. Calm Lark has been my friend. She makes the journey with her husband, Bold Hawk. She has been treated as his equal for all their years together. He took no other wife. Their love for each other is almost legend among the People. He will die soon, and she will be at his side. She will then wait her turn, or more likely, not to risk the separation of their spirits in the next life, she will take up her knife and join him quickly."

"You are saying she will kill herself?"

"She does not want to know a minute without him close by."

"Oh, my God. And these are the people our press and politicians call animals and savages? Creatures who have no feelings?"

No reply was expected. For an instant Jael's eyes locked with Josh's. The story of Calm Lark and Bold Hawk, almost at its conclusion, challenged her cynicism. Could life be more than survival and fleeting moments of happiness?

50

JOSH FELT SOME relief that the trek to Fort Sill and the reservation was not entirely a dismal trail and certainly did not approach the grueling, tragic journey of the infamous Cherokee Trail of Tears. The trip was little more than a week's time for men on horseback. It took the Kwahadi just short of a month to cover the same distance. Much of this was due to the weakness and half-starved condition of horses and people after a devastating winter. Also, many of the People were forced to walk the nearly two hundred miles to the reservation, and there were the burdens of possessions they had tried to salvage from the village, many of which were abandoned and marked their passing on the land as they were tossed aside.

No small number of the young and old died along the way. Some of the ancient ones simply chose to leave the sad parade and walk off into the endless prairie, to die like the others who departed before commencement of the trek. There were several small war parties who broke off from the scattered caravan, one led by Fights Many, boasting pledges to fight on. Their women and children would be at the reservation, however, Josh figured, and they would eventually show up there.

A good number of the travelers approached reservation life with high expectations. There were the optimists, whose spirits always convinced them life will soon be better. And there were the gullible, who foolishly believed the white man's lies of reservation paradise. And finally, there were the pragmatic realists, most notable among them, Quanah, who did not trust their former enemies but were determined to make the best of the life ahead and bend as much of it as possible to their own wills and cunning. Defeat was not a part of their mindsets. Josh was confident the others of Quanah's ilk would ultimately end up in his shadow. And Rivers and Sinclair would be there to help him—for a reasonable fee, of course.

Josh sat astride the strawberry roan gelding Rylee had sold him. She was vague about how she came to own the animal, and he hoped that a Comanche warrior did not see the large, thickly-muscled animal and lay claim to it as his own. The young horse had promise, but he was a bit skittish and contrary, in contrast to Buck, who had been gentle as a lap cat. He had not named the horse. He was superstitious about that right now, and deep down he thought it might be an act of disloyalty to Buck. The horse was not the attention-grabber of a stallion like Wolf's eerily-masked Owl, but Josh thought he would do in time.

As he watched the scattered and disorganized parade of Comanche trudge past, it seemed to him that for those Comanche who were not on the edge of death, they were dealing with this time as an extended party. Small parties rode out to hunt, usually with some success, for game. Occasionally, they came back with a buffalo or two and frequently with a doe or buck. The villagers were not so hungry now.

Patrols of soldiers could be seen watching over the proceedings in the distance, but they did not once interfere with the departures of Comanche from the main body. Mackenzie must have ordered them to stand down. A good start.

At evening there were the drum beats breaking the silence of the night and later came the old dances and chants and songs. He had watched as Michael and Jael participated in the festivities and later drew in Tabby and Rylee. Last night Jael had pulled him into the circle of dancers, and, after token resistance, he had joined them. The Comanche had roared with laughter at the booted dancer, and for a time he had been self-conscious and embarrassed, but, finally, as the others nodded approvingly, he gave in to it, and this morning could not recall the last time he had so much fun.

His reverie was interrupted when Tabby pulled her mare in beside him. "Big brother, how far are we from Sill?" she asked.

"I suppose it will take Quanah and the band another three or four days to get there, but I could ride it in less than a day."

"I want to ride in to see if I can interview Colonel Mackenzie, and, maybe, the Indian agent and some others before the Comanche arrive. I have a feeling they'll be hard to track down after their guests get there."

"I can ride ahead with you."

"Tomorrow morning we'll all ride to Sill. Jael wants to check on transportation arrangements. She'll stay around for a week in case Quanah needs her to interpret when they first come in, but then, one way or another, she and Rylee are heading to Denver."

"A week?"

"You heard me right, big brother. It's time to quit farting around."

51

WHEN THEY ARRIVED at Fort Sill mid-afternoon the next day, Jael had a sinking feeling in her stomach. She struggled to fight off panic that was trying to overtake her. She had not told Michael yet that she would be leaving him with his father and that he might not see her again for a long time—if ever. She would write, of course, and after a year or so, if Josh approved, one might visit the other on occasion. Those things would eventually be sorted out by time and events. How would she explain this? At least, he had come to know Joshua and accepted him as his father. The relationship was still tentative, but she knew it would be fine.

As they sauntered their horses onto the parade grounds, Josh said, "We can stay at the law firm's house. The work should be completed there by now." Josh led the way as they rode out to the stone house which reminded Jael of a small castle from her German childhood, standing like a lonely beacon on the plains. Josh pumped water from a cistern into a concrete tank for the horses, and, after the animals had drunk their fill, they hitched them under the roof of the small lean-to. Josh found keys under a flat rock near the corner of the stable where Wolf had said they would be.

Lugging their robes and gear, the party followed Josh into the house. Jael was surprised to find the huge kitchen-living area furnished, though sparsely. She traced her fingers over the oak table. She did not know about such things, but she thought it was beautiful and sturdy, yet simple in design,

Tabitha said, "I think Oliver built most of the furniture. He said he thought he and a sergeant cabinet maker would have to do most of the work. With all humility, I must say I gave him suggestions as to what would be needed."

They walked through the door of the law offices separated by a partition from the residential area. Josh rubbed his chin thoughtfully. "Two private offices off the outer reception area. I thought there would be one."

"I suggested two smaller offices, with each having floor to ceiling book shelves on one wall. It gives you room to grow," Tabitha said.

"It should work just fine."

Jael was uncomfortable with this. She sensed that Tabitha was in control of the agenda, and she did not know what to do about it. She followed the tour upstairs, hanging back from the others as she tried to plot the strategy for her exit. She heard Rylee and Michael chattering excitedly on the second floor. Since they had seemed bored and silent up to now, she hurried up the stairs.

"These are nicer than Grandma's!" Rylee squealed, as she grabbed Jael's hand and took her into a small bedroom with a single bed. "The other is just like it."

It was a small bedroom with a single window and an oak chest, with ample space for another item of furniture or two. "You should see the third room," Rylee said. "It's at the end of the hall."

Jael followed Riley, trying to subdue her own enthusiasm. She walked into a room twice the size of the other bedrooms, centered by a large double bed. There was a window on each side of the room, but it had not yet been otherwise furnished. One of the plastered walls was imprinted with markings of arrows, axes, animal tracks, buffalo and other characterizations symbolic of Comanche life. Tabitha and Joshua stood near one window, looking at her expectantly.

"It's beautiful," she said, "but strange."

Tabitha announced, "The kids and I are going downstairs. Josh, you and Jael are not allowed to come down until you have talked some things out."

What was Tabitha doing to her? Jael didn't know what to say. Thankfully, Josh rescued her.

"Sit down with me on the edge of the bed."

She sat down and he sat down close to her and wrapped his arm around her shoulders. The closeness, and his touch, was almost more than she could bear.

Josh said, "I think the mattress is down-filled. The others are straw."

"I would not know."

"We need to make some decisions."

"I thought they had been made."

"Decisions can be changed."

"Sometimes, I guess."

"There are two offices downstairs. One for each of us."

"I am not taking the job. It would not work."

"There is one bed here. I suppose we would have to share that."

"What are you saying?"

"I'm asking you to marry me, Jael Chernik or She Who Speaks, or whoever you are at this moment. I love you and I want to spend the rest of my days loving you. I realized that for certain when I saw Calm Lark and Bold Hawk. I want us to have a love that becomes a legend. Share my life with me. Let's raise our son together, and Rylee will be our daughter."

"I don't know what to say."

"One word will suffice."

"Yes." She turned and fell into his arms.

Epilogue

OSH WANTED TO find the post chaplain and marry Jael the same day he proposed, but she did not wish to marry until after Quanah arrived. She insisted, however, they would share the room and bed until that day came, and he raised no objection. A bride-to-be was entitled to some indulgence, was she not?

In the meantime, Tabitha snatched up enough interviews to fill ten issues of the *Daily New Mexican* and several chapters of her non-fiction book. As a bonus, she found the inspiration for her "happy ending" novel and eventually wrote The Last Hunt, one of the best-selling love stories of her time.

Josh and Jael agreed they would divide their time between Fort Sill and Santa Fe, where they would build a modest home. Jael would legally adopt Michael and would clerk with the law firm until she passed the bar exam and was admitted to practice as a full-fledged lawyer. They would offer to adopt Rylee, but she, of course, could choose her own path. Either way, she would be family.

Slightly over four hundred Kwahadi arrived at noon on June 2, 1875 at Signal Station, a few miles west of Fort Sill and three miles south of the Rivers and Sinclair office-residence. No chief or warrior was imprisoned in the ice house or elsewhere. The Comanche were required to surrender firearms but retained their other weapons. They were permitted to keep some of their horses, and most that were confiscated were later returned. No other tribe or band had ever been treated as well as Quanah's Kwahadi. That is not to suggest they would not face trials and tribulations in the months and years ahead.

Joshua Rivers and Jael Chernik Rivers were married by the army chaplain at their Fort Sill residence. Witnesses were their tipi family, Colonel Ranald Slidell Mackenzie and the Colonel's budding friend and ally, the man who would soon become known as Quanah Parker, the first Principal Chief of the Comanche.

Author's Note

This novel is a work of fiction, but the author has attempted to follow the historical path of the last Comanche surrender without taking undue literary license. Colonel Ranald Slidell Mackenzie, Indian Agent J.M. Haworth, Dr. Jacob J. Sturm, Wild Horse, Kicking Bird, Isa-tai and, of course, Quanah, are actual persons who left their footprints on the history of their times. I cannot vouch for She Who Speaks and the Rivers clan.

I wish to acknowledge the following reference works which were helpful in the writing of the novel:

S. C. Gwynne, EMPIRE OF THE SUMMER MOON. Scribner, 2010

Bill Neeley, THE LAST COMANCHE CHIEF. John Wiley & Sons, 1995

Ernest Wallace & E. Adamson Hoebel, THE COMANCHES: LORDS OF THE SOUTH PLAINS. University of Oklahoma Press, 1952

Pekka Hamalainen, COMANCHE EMPIRE. Yale University Press, 2008

W. S. Nye, CARBINE & LANCE: THE STORY OF OLD FORT SILL. University of Oklahoma Press, 1969 Revised

Duane F. Guy (Editor), THE STORY OF PALO DURO CANYON, Texas Tech University Press, 2001

Printed in Great Britain
by Amazon